Mission: Accomplished

A CLUB ALIAS NOVELLA COLLECTION

KD Robichaux

MISSION ACCOMPLISHED
Rendexvous
Karma's Pawn
Until We Meet Again

Editing by Hot Tree Editing
www.hottreeediting.com
Cover Design and
Formatting by Pink Ink Designs
www.pinkinkdesigns.com

Rendezvous:
This story contains elements of Aleatha Romig's copyrighted works that are part of her Infidelity Series, and it is published with the permission of Aleatha Romig, information about whose books are found at www.aleatharomig.com/infidelity-series.

Until We Meet Again:
KD Robichaux was granted permission by Aurora Rose Reynolds to use the copyrighted characters and/or worlds created by Aurora Rose Reynolds in the Original Work; all copyright protection to the characters and/or worlds of Aurora Rose Reynolds in the Original Works are and shall continue to be retained by Aurora Rose Reynolds. www.aurorarosereynolds.com

Also by KD Robichaux

THE BLOGGER DIARIES TRILOGY

Wished for You

Wish He Was You

Wish Come True

No Trespassing:

A Standalone Enemies-to-Lovers Romantic Adventure

Steal You:

A Standalone Dark Romance

CLUB ALIAS

Confession Duet Boxed Set (Contains Before the Lie and Truth Revealed)

Seven: A Club Alias Novel

Rendezvous: A Club Alias Novella

Karma's Pawn: A Club Alias Novella

Until We Meet Again: A Club Alias Novella

Doc: A Club Alias Novel (Coming Soon)

Knight: A Club Alias Novel (Coming Soon)

THE FIDELITY WORLD

RENDEZVOUS

chapter 1

"Brian Glover," Clarice singsongs as she answers after the second ring. "As I live and breathe, handsome."

"Hello, lover." I hear her sultry chuckle. She loves it when I call her that instead of her name. Understandable, seeing how most people greet her with a creepy lilt to their voice, mimicking a certain infamous fictional cannibalistic doctor. "What would you say if I told you I have a job in New York starting on Tuesday?"

Clarice hums. "I'd say I have to look at my schedule, like I always tell you, and then we'd play our little game of cat and mouse, where I play hard to get, all while I'm already packing my bag to come see you."

I can hear the smile in her voice, and in my mind I can see it as clearly as if she were sitting right beside me in the passenger seat of my SUV. "Atta girl. I'll be staying in Manhattan. Anything you need to shoot up there while I'm working? It'll be mostly the same as always, me disappearing overnight, maybe a few hours during the day."

"It's New York, Bri. A photographer's playpen. I'm sure I'll find something to take pictures of while you're off saving the world one security detail at a time," she purrs, and the admiration in her tone shoots straight from my ear to my cock. "Plus, my friend Lyra, who is also a photographer, lives up there and I haven't seen her in a while. I can chill with her if the Big Apple gets too boring."

"Sounds good. I'll text you the address of where we're staying. And Clarice?"

Her voice turns quiet, matching mine. "Yeah, Bri?"

"I've missed you," I confess.

She giggles, an attempt to make light of the depth of my words. "Well, I've missed you too, big guy. I can't wait to see you!" And with that, the line goes dead. The same way it always does when I try to tell Clarice the way I feel.

I set my phone in my cup holder then swipe my hand down my beard. "That woman," I murmur to myself.

For a couple of years now, anytime I go on an out-of-state mission, I always call Clarice and ask if she'd like to meet me there. We're not in a relationship, obviously. She likes to call us "besties with bennies," while I call her my "secret lover" just to hear the sweet sound of her laughter. And for now, I'll take what I can get from the raven-haired beauty. With my job, I don't really have time to put in the effort for a committed relationship anyway. But if I did, it would most certainly be with her.

We met years ago, while I was deployed in Afghanistan with the Army. She was an American photographer capturing breathtaking images of the war with her camera for a magazine. When I discharged and started working for my security company, we kept in touch. My first mission happened to be near where she worked, so we hooked up. She even took me to a local BDSM club when my mission was complete, and ever since, we've made a tradition out of it. She meets me where a job takes me, and when it's over, I get "rewarded for a job well done" by her treating me to her submission. New York will be a new one for us, and I can only imagine what a BDSM club in the world-famous city will be like. Surely, we can find one as high-end as the one I own with my three business partners. Clarice deserves nothing less.

I got the call about an hour ago. Doc, the head of our mercenary team—which is disguised as our security company—phoned to let me know there was a job up north. Since I'm the only one on my team who does out-of-state missions anymore, ever since they each found their other half, it's up to me to get the job done. I don't mind. I actually prefer getting out of our small military town and putting my skills to use. Regular security details get rather boring when you're used to being shot at in a war zone.

Apparently, I will be doing a job for a Mrs. Witt, who works for Demetri Security. For now, that's all I know until I can get to New York and have a sit-down meeting. I'm used to hush-hush situations, so the request isn't surprising.

I head home from the club, ready to pack and go to bed. Yet I don't know how much sleep I'll be able to get knowing I'll soon be sharing a bed with the only woman who's ever made me feel alive when I'm so used to being surrounded by death.

chapter 2

"BEFORE WE BEGIN, MR. GLOVER, I need you to sign these nondisclosure and confidentiality agreements," Mrs. Witt, a short woman with a blunt, chin-length haircut, tells me, sliding the contracts across the desk, where I sit inside her office in New York. I scrawl my name across the lines, dating them before setting the pen down and returning them to her side of the lacquered surface. "Very good. Welcome to Infidelity. On the outside, we are a Fortune 500 company that employs hundreds of people, from writers and photographers to janitorial personnel," she states, sounding like she's given this spiel many times before.

"But on the inside?" I prompt, resting my ankle on the opposite knee as I sit back in the leather chair.

"We create companionship opportunities. I say 'we,' but really, I don't work for Infidelity, but rather its main investor, Demetri

Enterprises. It is my job, as head of security, to make sure all of my employer's assets remain that way, an asset, rather than a liability."

"*You're* the head of security?" I ask, unable to hide the surprise from my tone. The woman is a tiny little thing and looks to be almost two decades older than me.

Her face turns blank. "Yes. I am the brains, not the brawn. Obviously, they hired me to do the thinking, since men are only good for doing neck-down work." She smirks.

"Touché," I mumble, taking the jab since I had let the offensive outburst slip.

She nods once, her eyes sparkling with humor. "I have a background in the CIA and give even the best hackers in the world a run for their money. There's only one person I know of who can find information faster than me, a literal genius who got his masters at MIT when he was just a teenager. I understand Seth Owens works with you at your security company." She smiles, a look people usually get when talking about the "class clown" of our business.

"That he does," I confirm, and she nods again.

"His talent is astounding. He's actually the reason you're here. When I called him for assistance, he said you would be the man for the job."

"And what is the job exactly?" I question, wanting to move this along so I can get started… and get to the hotel suite before Clarice arrives.

"In order to tell you that, I need to explain what Infidelity *really* is. As I was saying, we create opportunities for companionship. It is sort of like an escort service, but we do not solicit sex. An Infidelity employee sets up a profile, and then a client can hire them by agreeing to a one-year contract. Well, not really a contract, but for lack of a better word. The employee's profile is very detailed. They set their limits, what they are willing and unwilling to do, what they themselves are looking for in a companion, what they do in their life, all to make the most perfect match." She reaches into a drawer and pulls out a file, flipping it open. Inside is a picture of a blonde woman with a pleasant smile on her face, along with a printed version of what looks like an online dating site profile.

"Missing, dead, or both?" I ask, my face turning grim.

"Just missing. She was alive as of this morning. Quincy Herald has been the companion of billionaire hotelier Jean LaRue for the past year. At the one-year mark, the employee and the client are able to renew their companionship if they mutually agree. Quincy decided not to re-up for another year, because she had earned enough money to start her own business—the reason she signed on with Infidelity in the first place. Mr. LaRue wasn't happy with her decision and took it upon himself to make her stay," she explains, and I shift in my seat, sitting up to lean over the file.

"And how do you know he's taken her against her will? Maybe she wanted to stay with him, and they're off just having a romantic getaway or some shit," I prompt.

"Because the employee is always contacted separately from the client when it comes time to renew the agreement. I personally interviewed Quincy, and she was very adamant that she was not going to sign up for another year, because she was excited to finally start her bakery. They were finishing up the final three days of the one-year agreement. She had an appointment at a location to sign all the closing contracts on her storefront, but she never showed. When she wouldn't answer her phone, her sister got scared. She's also an Infidelity employee, so she knew the truth of what was going on and called us to look into it."

"So there is no doubt this rich douche has taken her against her will. How do you know she was alive this morning?" I question.

"We got a call on the Infidelity emergency line. It was too quick to trace, but she was able to get out that she was in one of his hotels and had not been taken out of the country. We have reason to believe she is actually still in the state." She taps out a few keystrokes on her laptop and then spins it around for me to see. "There has been no movement of Mr. LaRue's private jet, no activity to indicate travel by other airlines. The only thing we've caught is footage of him forcibly leading her out to his garage at his Staten Island hotel and them getting into his car before leaving. We had our team watching the security cameras for his other hotels in the state so we could see if they arrived at one and we could go get her, but unfortunately, twenty minutes after they left the island, all security footage went black."

"He turned off all the cams in all his hotels," I state.

"Yes."

"Well fuck."

"Yep."

"All right. I'll get Seth on top of this. There's nothing really I can do until we find out where she is. But if y'all find her, no one can get her out of there more safely than I can. I'm your best shot at her getting out of this alive," I state. I'm not cocky; it's the truth. I'm the person on the team they always call for situations like this. Even though I tower over my three coworkers, I'm the stealthiest but also the most levelheaded. I'm able to control my emotions when put under pressure. I've perfected the art of keeping myself somewhat disconnected. I know I come across as a heartless asshole most of the time, but it makes me damn good at my job.

"All right. Thank you, Mr. Glover," Mrs. Witt replies.

"Just Glover is fine, ma'am."

She nods, shaking my hand as we stand. "You can take the file with you, and I have all of your contact information from Seth. So if we get any news, I'll call you ASAP."

chapter 3

"BRI, MY MAN! YOU MAKE IT TO New York okay?" Seth hollers into the phone, trying to be heard over the thumping music of our club. A few seconds later, the bass dulls to a low throb in the background, and I imagine he's gone upstairs to the offices, closing the door behind him.

"Yeah. Got to the hotel about an hour ago and ate some dinner. Did Mrs. Witt contact you?" I ask.

"Yes. Not much to go off, but I've got all systems running, watching all his credit card activity. I've tapped into a few of his vehicles' GPS systems, but haven't been able to locate the one he's apparently using. Fucker has over a dozen. Who the fuck needs that many cars?" he gripes.

I roll my eyes. "Says the dude who doesn't own one."

"Hey, I have my bike. And we have Twyla's car too. We don't

need more than that. Especially since I switched out my single seat for a double on the motorcycle. You can't beat the feel of a woman's legs wrapped around yours while you're riding, and when you shift and her titties press against your back—" I hear a smack and Seth call out "Ouch, woman! Today was chest day at the gym. Watch the pecs."

"Stop talking about my boobs with Glover," I hear Twyla hiss in the background.

Seth sighs into the phone. "Anyway, yeah. Bike beats a car any day of the week. But this bag of dicktips has fourteen. It'll take me a few more hours to find all the VIN numbers and tap into the rest of the systems. According to Mrs. Witt, the car in the surveillance footage looked like a newer model sedan, so I'll check those out first. But he could've switched cars after the cameras went black."

"Okay, just call me as soon as you get a lead. I'm kind of wandering around aimlessly until y'all tell me where to go," I say, looking up as there's a tap on the hotel room door.

"Will do, bud," Seth replies, and we hang up.

I get up off the edge of the bed and force myself to walk to the door calmly, when everything inside me is telling me to run to the woman I know is behind it. When I pull it open, my heart thunders behind my ribcage when I see her beautiful smile spread across her face. "Hello, lover," I greet quietly, and brace myself when she makes her move.

She drops her bags there in the doorway and launches herself into my arms, uncaring she's in a skirt, knocking me back a single step as I wrap my arm around her hips. Even though she's curvy in all the right places, with my wingspan, I'm able to circle her entire body with one arm while I keep the door open with the other. With her bare legs wrapped around my hips, she grasps behind my neck and leans back to look into my eyes. "Hey, big guy. How's the air up here?" she teases, like she always does before sliding down my six-foot, eight-inch frame.

With the top of her head now at my chest level, she has to tilt way back in order to look up at me, so I take the opportunity to lace my fingers through the back of her hair, my large hand cupping her skull. She's so tiny. I could crush her easily just by making a fist, yet she brings out a gentleness in me that has me handling her like the precious piece of art she is. "Much better now that you're here," I murmur, before lowering my face to hers. She goes up on her tiptoes as I let go of the door and wrap my arm around the small of her back. My body surrounds hers as our lips connect.

And just like always, it's like coming home after a yearlong deployment. How such a little creature could hold a big man like me in the palm of her hand, I'll never know, but that's the way she makes me feel. Her kiss is fiery, even as it sends a soothing coolness down my spine, like walking into air conditioning after riding in a blistering Humvee all day. She's like a cold glass of water after sweating in the desert for weeks, like the first time I kissed her in Afghanistan. She quenches a thirst inside me that no amount of submissives at my club could ever slake. It's why I don't bother fucking anyone there, even being one of the head Doms. Why would I when I'd only be picturing Clarice in their place? And everything about that just feels wrong.

With a sweet sigh of satisfaction, she gently breaks the kiss, pulling back and looking behind her at her bags while I try to calm the thundering of my heart. "I guess we better get my bags in so we can close the door all the way. Don't want to give anyone a show," she says on a giggle.

"Why not? We've done it before," I remind her, thinking back to the scenes we've done at various BDSM clubs around the country.

"Uh-uh, big guy. You haven't completed your mission. No reward for you… yet." She winks, spinning in my arms to bend over and grab the straps of her bags, her ass pressing to my front, and I nearly go cross-eyed.

I reach around her and take the bags from her hands, carrying them into the suite. Placing them on the luggage rack inside the closet, I then turn around to see her plop down on the end of the bed, he breasts bouncing at the top of her low-cut white T-shirt. She'll be the death of me.

"Nice place they put you up at this time. Come over here and tell mama about your mission," she says, reaching her arms out to me and opening and closing her hands.

I narrow my eyes at her. "I signed a nondisclosure." I shrug teasingly. "I can't *willingly* tell you a thing." I saunter toward her, and she takes my hand with one of her outstretched ones and yanks. She wouldn't really make me even budge, but I allow myself to fall onto the mattress on my back and smirk as she climbs on top of me.

"I can torture it out of you," she whispers, leaning forward until her chest is pressed to mine. My eyes can't decide which they'd rather focus on, the red pout of her perfect lips or her breasts now spilling from her neckline. My cock swells almost painfully inside my jeans. "Mmm, feels like someone likes that idea." She grinds her hips, pressing her smoldering core down on top of my erection.

"Fuck, baby. Please," I groan, both loving and hating the fact she's the only woman who can make me beg. The urge to close my eyes and just feel her comes over me, but I don't want to look away from her. There've been too many long nights I've spent dreaming about her face to not keep my gaze locked on her while she's actually here, in my presence, mounting me and bringing me to my knees the way only she can.

She sits up abruptly, reaching for my belt, and I sigh in relief that she's giving in so easily. She usually likes to tease me for hours before finally giving me a real taste of her. But that relief comes to a halt at her wicked grin. I lift my hips slightly, allowing her to pull the belt free from the loops when she tugs, my brow furrowing in confusion.

She purses her lips in a sexy taunt before lifting a perfectly arched eyebrow. "Aww, you didn't think it'd be that easy, did you, big guy?" she purrs, and she loops the belt around my wrists, tightening the leather until my hands are locked together above my head.

I could get out of it easily, but I don't want to. I love it when she toys with me like this. She's the only one I play this game with, the sole person in the entire world I trust enough to give my own submission to. I may be a Dom, but for her, for my Clarice, I become a switch. It does something for my soul that I can't explain, and I know it does the same for her, something we never talk about, something she's never opened up to me about in all the years we've been friends and have taken turns letting the other dominate.

"Now," she chirps, reaching for the hem of her tee and peeling the tight material over her head. My Adam's apple moves in my throat as I swallow audibly. So goddamn perfect. "What's your mission, soldier?" She starts with the top button of my flannel and begins unfastening each one.

"I-uh… I have to rescue a chick who's been kidnapped. She uh…" I gulp when she finishes with the flannel and reaches for the button of my jeans. God, she makes me so weak. "She was something of an escort, a companion. And her sugar daddy didn't like it when she told him she wanted to end things." I signed a non-disclosure agreement, so I'll keep my mouth shut about Infidelity, but I trust Clarice and know she'll keep the details I confide in her to herself.

She tugs down my zipper. "He abused her?"

My hips instinctively lift to press against her heat. "None that was reported."

She hops off me, and I fight back a whimper at the loss of her touch. She may make me weak, but I'll be damned if I fucking whimper like a little bitch. I lift my head to watch her as she unlaces my boots and pulls them from my feet along with my socks. And then I rock from side to side as she tugs on my jeans, allowing her to yank them down my legs before they disappear. She reaches behind her, unfastening her bra before letting it fall to the floor, and then she hovers over me and begins to slide her tits from my ankles, all the way up to the tops of my thighs, my hairy legs turning her puffy pink nipples into hard little points.

"Are there any leads?" she breathes along the elastic of my boxer briefs before grasping hold of it with her teeth.

I gulp before replying, "None yet." She tugs the fabric over my aching cock. "Fuck, baby." I long to flip her over and bury myself deep inside her wet, molten core, but instead, I bask in the sweetness of surrendering to her wants. I'm sure it's an amazing feeling for her, for such a giant of a man to submit, knowing she has so much power over me. And I love the fact I can make her feel powerful, that I can do all that for her just by receiving the pleasure she wants to give me.

"Then whatever will we do to pass the time?" she asks, fake worry contorting her features as she stands at the foot of the bed after baring me from the waist down.

As if to answer her, my cock juts upward on its own, and the sound of her sweet giggle fills the room.

"Aww, does somebody want some attention?" She pouts as her eyes lock on my pulsing erection.

"Please," I groan, a single milky drop of precum oozing from the tip.

"Poor baby. He's crying," she whispers, her eyes showing sorrow as she crawls up my body once more. "Maybe I should kiss him to make him feel better."

I nod, unable to speak as I look down my body, her braced above my hips, her eyes never breaking contact with mine as she leans down and swipes her tongue up my length. I hiss as if she's burned me with her fiery touch, and the sound makes her grin impishly. She grasps hold of my steeled cock and engulfs the head with her searing mouth, and it takes everything in me not to thrust deeper. I learned my lesson the last time I wasn't able to control my instincts. She stopped and wouldn't continue for a full day, after making me promise I wouldn't jack off. And I'd never break a promise to Clarice, so it was pure torture until she gave me relief twenty-four hours later.

She releases my cock with a pop, smiling up at me. "Such a good boy," she purrs, and then straddles me. She takes my shaft in her tight fist before lining me up with her dripping heat beneath her skirt. I hadn't realized until now that she's not wearing any underwear. The knowledge is equally hot as it is infuriating, but I force myself to remain in my submission. I will have to scold her later for going around without panties on, when a draft of air at the right angle could bare her to someone's eyes... someone's that aren't mine.

But for now, I close my eyes and savor the feeling of my length disappearing inch by slow inch as she lowers herself until she has me fully seated inside her. And then she begins to move, and I lose all sense of the world except for the places where our bodies are joined together to become one.

She rides me with vigor, her movements desperate as she chases her orgasm, the look on her impossibly gorgeous face telling me she is so close she can almost taste it. I know I could get her there if she'd allow me to touch her, but she hasn't released my hands, indicating she doesn't want me to break from my surrender.

She drops herself so hard I feel the head of my dick punch against her cervix, and as she grinds herself in circles, my vision goes blurry at how goddamn perfect she feels. My breath comes out in pants as I try to stave off my orgasm, refusing to blow my load until my beautiful mistress has gotten her blissful release.

Her movements turn jerky, less graceful as her face contorts with her concentration. And finally, "Now, Bri!" leaves her on a panicked whimper as her body folds in on itself, her face planting against my chest as I feel her walls tighten around me in a viselike grip. The pressure valve inside me releases and I come so hard I'm scared the power behind my orgasm will hurt her. So I try to be as still as possible while my cock pulses, emptying jet after jet of cum inside her, as she melts on top me.

"Damn, big guy," she sighs against my chest, her hot breath tickling my nipple. "That never gets old."

I chuckle beneath her, then work my hands out of the belt, my arms coming down around her to hold her against me as I roll her until I'm on top, my cock still firmly planted inside her depths. "I have no doubt it ever would with you, lover," I tell her, leaning down to rub my nose against hers.

She allows herself a split second of the dreamy look in her eyes before she blinks it away, changing the subject. "So what's your plan of attack for rescuing this girl?"

"Tonight, I'm going to make a few stops at some of the hotels he owns, see if anyone has seen him around. Hopefully, Seth will have something pop up in all his computer sorcery that will give me something to go on," I tell her, and slide gently out of her, watching her wince. "You okay? Did I hurt you?"

She smiles up at me sleepily. "Technically, I would've hurt myself. I was the one bouncing around on your disco stick. But I'm fine. It's just been a while… and God blessed you."

I chuckle, moving to the bathroom to wet a washcloth with hot water. When I return to her, she spreads her knees for me, and I press the steaming cotton to her swollen flesh. She loves it when I do this for her, claiming she'd never been taken care of after sex before she met me. For me though, aftercare is one of the best parts of making love to her. It's one of the only times she allows me to treat her like the queen I see her as.

"You know, the first time I met you, I wondered if you were going to be an Elliot Richards situation." She grins.

"Who the hell is Elliot Richards?" I ask, jealousy evident in my voice.

"Elliot Richards, in *Bedazzled*. The part when Brendan Fraser uses one of his wishes to become a basketball player. He's huge, like seven feet tall, and the chick he's in love with is a sports reporter. She follows him into the locker room to seduce him, thinking his wang is going to match the rest of his giant frame," she explains, her grin still in place.

"And did it?" I prompt, removing the cloth and positioning my shoulders between her legs.

She glances down her delicious body to meet my eyes as I take a long, slow swipe up her folds, flattening my tongue against her and allowing the heat of my mouth to soak into her abused flesh, soothing her.

"No. He had a micropenis, and when he saw it, he started yelling 'Damn the devil! Damn the devil to hell!' Because she—the devil, I mean—kept messing up his wishes," she rambles, never looking away from my gaze. It's the only hint I get that I affect her the same way she affects me.

The pure eroticism of staring into each other's eyes while I gently eat her pussy has me hardening once more, but feeling how swollen she is, I won't take her again tonight. If she hasn't had sex since the last time we met up, then it's been a little over a month. But that's not something we discuss. We have a mutual respect and trust for each other. We really are each other's best friend. We know the other is clean, and she is on birth control, and we promised we're the only ones we'd not use a condom with.

"So you were already thinking about the size of my dick the

first time you met me?" I murmur against her slick folds, and her hips make a circle against my lips.

"Big guy, I'm sure that's what *all* women think when they first meet you. 'I wonder if his cock matches the rest of him,'" she mocks the last part in a valley girl voice. "Bitches," she adds under her breath, and a smile spreads across my face at her slip of jealousy.

"And does it?" I prompt, just to egg her on as I circle her clit with the tip of my tongue.

She bites her lip, her brow furrowing in pleasure, before she attempts to redeem her sassiness. "You fishing for compliments, Jolly Green?" Her head then presses back against the mattress as her hands shoot into my hair when I nip at her bundle of sensitive nerves before sucking it into my mouth, releasing her with a loud sound of suction.

"I just love hearing you talk, beautiful. And even more when it's about my cock," I tell her, and then stop messing around. I set upon her pussy like a starved man, eating her with fervor until she's a writhing, drenched mess beneath me. When her inner thighs tremble, I know she's about to come, so I put all the focus on her clit until she explodes.

She cradles my head against her, holding me there as if her life depends on it. And I savor this perfect moment, the few seconds when she's vulnerable and her walls come down, and bask in the fact I'm the one she's hanging onto.

chapter 4

AFTER TUCKING CLARICE BENEATH THE sheets in the king-size bed, I dress and head out for some recon. I start with LaRue Hotel Manhattan, since it's the closest. Walking into the lobby through the rotating doors, I move to the concierge desk.

"Bonjour, monsieur," the man in uniform greets me. "How may I assist you?"

I pull the picture of Quincy, which I'd taken from the folder, out of my back pocket and hold it up to face him. "Have you seen this woman? She's been reported missing," I ask, and watch his face carefully.

He takes the photo from my hand and looks closely. "She… this is Mademoiselle Herald," he replies, his French accent thick. "She is missing?" His confused eyes lift to meet mine.

"Yes. When was the last time you saw her?" I question. I study his microexpressions, seeing his eyes stare straight ahead as he thinks back, so I know he's actually trying to remember instead of thinking up a lie.

"Two… no three days ago. Today is Tuesday, and I believe it was Saturday when I saw her having breakfast in the restaurant with Monsieur LaRue. Is he the one who reported her missing?" the concierge asks worriedly.

"I'm not at liberty to answer that question during the investigation," I reply. "So you have not seen her since then?"

"No, sir." He shakes his head. "Come to think of it, I have not seen Monsieur LaRue since then either. They're usually attached at the hip."

"Thank you for answering my questions. If you see either Mr. LaRue or Ms. Herald, please contact me at this number." I hand him a card with my cell number on it. "This investigation is a private one, so please keep all of this to yourself," I tell him, hoping for just the opposite. If word gets back to Jean LaRue that someone was here at this location looking for him, he'll be less likely to move here, knocking off a hiding spot from the long list.

As I exit the hotel, stepping out on the mostly empty sidewalk, since it's nearly 10:00 p.m., I grab my cell out of my pocket as it begins to ring. Seeing it's Seth, I hope for good news. "What you got?" I greet.

"Bruh, you got a letter in your mailbox. Might want to pick that wedgie," he replies, and my hand shoots to my ass.

"I do not, fuckface. Is there a point to your call?" I growl, looking behind me.

"Just kidding. But you might want to fix your sex hair before questioning anyone else. Kinda hard to find you an intimidating authority figure when you look like you just got done letting someone ride you like a pony," Seth informs me, and I reach up to comb my fingers through my dark blond hair.

"So I take it you've been able to hack into their surveillance systems?" I prompt, wondering about the location of the camera he's currently watching me from.

"I'm having to go inside each hotel's cameras and turn them back on, while also making sure to keep the images from showing up on the monitors in their security rooms. I know, I know. I'm a badass motherfucker," he boasts.

I roll my eyes. "Yeah, yeah. Anyway, the concierge I just questioned seemed genuinely surprised when I told him about our missing person. No shiftiness. If he had seen her or his employer and tried to hide the fact from me, I would've been able to spot it. He said he hadn't seen either of them since Saturday at breakfast. So this location can be crossed off the list."

"One down, a couple to go. Well, hotels anyway. God only knows where they could be if he's somewhere else," Seth mumbles.

"True story. But in the update you e-mailed me, it looks like he doesn't have any other residences. He just lives in the penthouses at each of his hotels." I glance at my watch, walking over to the valet to retrieve my SUV, handing him my ticket.

"Let's just hope he's spending the time trying to convince her to stay by lavishing her with gifts and luxury while whispering sweet nothings. I like that option much more than the idea of her being held prisoner and him doing... not so nice things to her." His voice quiets on the last part, probably thinking back to what happened to his wife, Twyla.

The valet pulls up with my SUV, and I hand him a tip as I switch places with him. "There was no history of violence. No reports against this Jean LaRue guy. In his profile for Infidelity, he didn't even put BDSM or rough sex as one of his interests. In fact, even in Quincy's profile, it says she would prefer a platonic companionship behind closed doors. They wouldn't have matched her with this guy if that wasn't something he was down with. Unless he thought he could convince her otherwise, thinking he would enjoy the chase and challenge of it all."

"God only knows, bro. I'll keep working my magic here though, and you keep doing your thing. Let me know if anyone seems suspicious and I'll dig into their background," he tells me.

"Will do," I reply, pulling out onto the street. "Talk to you later."

I hang up before he finishes singing, hearing only one line of *NSYNC's "Bye, Bye, Bye" before the blissful sound of silence fills my car.

I spend the next several hours making my way to each of Jean LaRue's hotels around the city, questioning employees on if they'd seen him or Quincy. Everyone's answers were the same; no one had spotted them in the past few days. They seemed to have disappeared off the face of the earth, and I was starting to believe they were either not at one of his properties, or they had made it out of state by car. The only thing that made me think they were still around though was the fact he hadn't used any of his credit cards. Yes, he could easily have a pile of cash lying around to grab before they left, but they hadn't been spotted on any type of traffic cams or anything. I was still waiting for Seth to find out which car of LaRue's they took so he could track either the GPS or the license plate number.

Until then, as the sun starts to rise over the horizon, I decide to go get some shuteye with the vixen currently sleeping in my bed.

chapter 5

"WHAT DID YOU DO LAST NIGHT, BEAUTIFUL?" I murmur, as I crawl up Clarice's relaxed body. She stirred when I had entered our hotel room moments ago, stretching her arms above her head, her tits pressing against the soft fabric of my white tee she must've put on before going to sleep.

Eyes still closed, she put her hand over her mouth as she spoke. "I sat at the café across the street and snapped some pretty cool photos while people watching. Come no closer if you want to live, Bri. My morning breath will kill you."

"I can think of worse ways to die," I tell her, removing her hand and kissing her deeply.

She gives in for a few seconds before she pushes at my chest, and I let her wiggle her way out from under me as she dances over to the bathroom. From my view from the bed, I can see her shapely legs and the roundness of her perfect ass peeking out from beneath my shirt as she bends over the sink, brushing her teeth quickly.

She prances back to me on her toes before hopping onto the bed on her knees beside me. "Wanna see?" she asks.

I reach for the bottom of the shirt, saying, "I always wanna see." But she bats my hand away, giggling.

"The pictures I took, silly," she clarifies, and I grin, placing my hands behind my head on the pillow as I enjoy the hopeful look in her eyes.

"Of course I do," I reply, and she squeaks as she reaches across me to the nightstand, where her camera is resting. With her knees on one side of my body, while she balances on one arm on the other side as she stretches for her equipment, I can't help my wandering hand as I slide it up the back of her thigh, palming the luscious globe of her ass. I massage the healthy amount of meat there, seeing her arm holding her up give out momentarily before she catches herself. I smirk to myself, knowing my touch affects her, before she sits up on her knees and swats my hand away.

She scoots until she's lying cuddled up close to my side, her head using my bicep as a pillow as I place my hand back behind my head. She pushes a few buttons on the black camera, and the big screen on the back of it below the viewfinder glows to life.

"Wanna play a game?" she purrs, and I turn my face to rest my nose at the top of her head, breathing in her scent.

"What kind of game?"

"It's a game Lyra and I play when we're being creepers. We make up stories about the people who pass by. We played it last night as I was snapping these pictures, so it'll be interesting to hear what you see when you look at the person in the shot," she explains.

I smile against her hair. She's the only person who can get me to slow down enough to lie around and play a silly game, especially when I have an open case to handle. She doesn't even have to try to force me, either. I agree willingly, without a struggle, just because it's something she wants from me. If Clarice wants to play a game, by God, I'm gonna play that damn game as long as she wants. Anything to spend time with her and make her happy.

"Okay, how about this guy?" she prompts, showing me a photo of a man in his late twenties dressed in a tuxedo. She zooms in a couple of clicks, and I see he's holding an umbrella over a woman's head as she gets into a yellow taxi.

"Hm. They're going to an opera, or more likely a Broadway show, seeing how we're in New York. He doesn't really want to see it, but if he wants to get under that expensive skirt she's wearing, he has to put in the effort," I answer.

She chuckles. "We said he was her kept man, seeing how she looks to be quite a few years older than him."

"Good one." I nod, and watch her flip to the next picture.

"All right, this lady." She zooms in again. This woman is in a black trench coat carrying a black leather bag. Her dark hair is sleek, falling almost to her ass.

"Dominatrix. She's on her way inside the hotel to meet up with her pudgy, hairy John who has hired her to walk on him with her stilettos while telling him he's a bad little boy," I reply, and she lowers the camera to her chest as her head tilts back and she bursts into laughter.

"Oh my God. That is so close to what I said! I instantly thought of Angelina Jolie in *Mr. and Mrs. Smith.*" She turns her head enough to look me in the eyes briefly before hers fall to my lips. I lean over and press a gentle kiss against hers, and then pull away, indicating the camera with a chin lift.

"What else you got?" I ask, and she smiles, obviously loving that I'm playing her game with enthusiasm.

"Here's a good one. What about this couple? We had a juicy story for them," she questions eagerly, flipping to another picture and zooming in.

They're directly across the street from where she sat at the café, which means they were at the entrance to the hotel where we're currently staying. Their bodies are half hidden behind a car as it passes by. The woman looks so familiar. She's wearing a simple but well-fitted gray dress, and her hair is in a ponytail. Her face is clean of all makeup, and she's very pretty. But it's when I take a closer look at the man that I realize who they are. The man is in a nice tailored suit. His hair is perfectly quaffed, and his beard is groomed to the point it looks painted on his face.

Jean LaRue and Quincy Herald.

"Holy fuck!" I sit up abruptly, pulling the camera out of her hands and pushing the button I saw her using to zoom in on the photo.

"What is it?" Clarice asks, her voice full of concern.

"Baby. Holy shit. That's them! That's who I've been looking for. She's the missing person, and he's the guy who kidnapped her," I say excitedly, hopping out of bed and grabbing my cell from the nightstand, where I'd set it before crawling into bed with her.

"Well, that's definitely not the juicy story we had for them," she gripes, pouting as she plops back on the pillow as I call Seth.

"What's up, man?" he answers, sounding groggy.

"I need you to get out of bed and hustle over to your spaceship," I tell him, referring to the giant computer setup he has in his apartment.

"On it." I hear the rustling of sheets as he hurries out of his bed, and I vaguely hear Twyla asking if he's okay. "Everything's fine, doll. Go back to sleep," he tells her, and then the sound of his computer chair being rolled back fills my ear. "Okay, what you need?"

"The hotel I'm at, the Fleur de Lis Hotel in Manhattan. What can you tell me about it?"

He types rapidly, and after a minute says, "Son of a bitch."

"What?" I bark, my adrenaline pumping through my system.

"It's not public record, so I had to do something not quite legal. But it's a boutique hotel owned by none other than Jean LaRue," he replies, and I set the camera down on the mattress before pointing a finger at Clarice, giving her a grin before jerking my fist back in a silent *Yes!*

"How the hell did we not know this shit?" I ask Seth.

"We only searched for LaRue Hotels and Suites, because that's the only thing they had in the information from his profile. It doesn't come up as a place of residence for him. And the way I had to dig, it's like he kept it as a secret location. A hideaway," he explains, all the while typing on his keyboard. "Motherfucker. There he is!"

"What?" I bark again, hating I can't see what he's pulled up on his screen.

"Tapped into the surveillance. Guess he didn't think he needed to turn them off here if it was unknown he owned the place. He's there... and..." He continues to type. "Looks like they're in room 703."

"Got it. Thanks, Seth," I say, and hang up. Hurrying to the foot of the bed, I pull my boots back on and quickly tie them. I move over to the safe in the closet and punch in my code, pulling my handgun out and tucking it in the back of my jeans.

"What's happening?" Clarice asks, sitting up on the bed, her face showing an uncharacteristic amount of worry I'm not used to seeing on her.

I take two strides, reaching her and wrapping my arm around her lower back. I pull her to me in one scoop, her soft front molding to my hardness. "You found her, baby. You saved her," I tell her, and I kiss her fiercely before letting her go and moving toward the door. "She's here, in this hotel. Right under our goddamn noses."

"Can't you... like, call the police or something?" Her voice is small, and it makes me turn back to face her.

My brow furrows as I take in her uncomfortable expression. "It's all right, lover. This is what I do. You know this. I'm invincible, remember?"

She smiles weakly, then forces out a laugh, waving her worry away. "Of course. I'm being silly. I must be close to pluggin' or something, going all girly on you."

I stride back over to her and engulf her with my large frame. "I like it when you worry about me, beautiful. Be as girly as you want. But I promise nothing's gonna happen to me." I rock her back and forth for a few moments until I feel her relax. I hear her breathe in my scent where her head rests on my chest, and I kiss the top of her head.

"You're my best friend, Bri. Don't go gettin' dead, okay?" she whispers.

"I won't. Gotta live in order to get my reward for a job well done." I pull back and wink, making her smile.

"Okay. Well then, go save the day, big guy," she orders, and I smack a kiss to her lips before turning and hurrying out the door.

chapter 6

I ENTER THE ELEVATOR, REACHING FOR THE seventh floor button. The doors close, and I immediately reach behind me, pulling my gun out of the back of my waistband. I hold it behind my thigh in case the doors open, and someone is standing there waiting for the elevator, but as soon as I see the hallway is clear, I lift my .45 and silently make my way to room 703. It's the only room on this end of the hall, indicating it must be huge—a suite.

Pressing my ear to the door, I hear nothing inside, so I hurriedly take out my wallet with one hand, continuing to train the gun on the door while I slip out the key card Seth gave me that supposedly opens any electronic lock. I replace my wallet in my back pocket, and exhale a breath, centering myself before sliding the card into the lock, sending up a silent prayer that it works. As soon as the tiny light turns green, with lightning-fast movements, I open the door, bursting into the room with my gun aimed ahead of me.

The room, set up like a living room's sitting area from what I can make out in the darkness, is empty, so I hurry over to the white door I see at the far end of the right wall. Getting closer, I see it has been barricaded by a door jammer. Whoever is inside wouldn't be able to get out because of the long metal pole lodged between the doorknob and the floor.

I remove it easily, turning the knob and opening the door.

The small figure groggily sits up in the middle of the bed, her disheveled appearance visible from the light coming from the bathroom over to the right.

She rubs her eyes, squinting. "Jean? It's so early. You okay?" she murmurs, and it confuses the fuck out of me. Why would she be worrying if her kidnapper is all right? The moment she registers I am not Jean LaRue, I see it in her eyes as her expression turns to terror when she spots my hulking frame with the gun trained on her, and she lets out a blood-curdling scream.

At the exact same time, something hits me from behind, and I stumble forward. Thankfully, whoever hit me must be short, because the object didn't connect with my head at my towering height, so I turn and aim my gun at the dark silhouette still inside the bedroom door.

"Get your fucking hands up," I growl loudly, and I hear Quincy gasp behind me.

"Please! Don't hurt him. We'll give you whatever you want.

Money? We have lots in the safe. Please, just don't hurt him," she begs, and it confuses me even more.

Gun still trained on LaRue, I hiss over my shoulder, "I'm not here to rob you. I'm fucking rescuing you."

"What?" she squeaks.

"Mon dieu," I hear LaRue sigh, and I see him shake his head.

"I was hired by Demetri Security to find and rescue you from the man keeping you captive, your Infidelity client, Jean LaRue," I explain briskly, my eyes darting between Quincy and the hotelier as I back up toward the bathroom so I can see both of them.

Silence.

And then, "I told you, Jean. I told you they would come looking for us. You should've trusted me. You should still... trust me." Quincy's voice is reassuring as she continues, "Your secrets are safe with me. Not only because of the contracts I signed, but because we're friends. For a whole year you've been my very best friend. You know in your heart I won't tell a soul."

With that, LaRue falls to his knees as he buries his face in his hands. That's when I see the man standing behind him in the doorway, still in the darkness of the living room. I raise my gun to aim at him, and he squeaks femininely and puts his hands up.

"Okay, what the *fuck* is going on?" I call fiercely.

"Please, sir. There's no need for the gun. I swear I'm safe," Quincy says quietly, scooting to the edge of the bed to stand, her hands coming up in a placating gesture.

"You were barricaded inside the room, ma'am," I remind her,

switching my weight from one foot to the other, not knowing exactly what to do. I'm so thrown off by their exchange and the sobbing man on the floor that I don't know what my next move should be. So, I lower my weapon, deciding to trust the woman as she moves to kneel in front of LaRue and wraps her arms around his shaking shoulders.

"Sir, come into the room so I can see you," I call out to the man in the doorway, and he enters timidly, his narrow, hairless chest coming into view before I see he has a sheet wrapped around his waist. And that's when everything clicks.

Her profile stating she wanted only a platonic relationship behind closed doors.

A secret she promises she won't tell.

"You're his beard," I murmur, and all three sets of eyes come to me, LaRue's wet from his tears, Quincy's full of worry, and the other man's wide, holding a hint of… jealousy?

"Please. No one can know. If anyone were to find out, he'd lose everything. His family will disown him," she pleads. The looks on all their faces would be heartbreaking if I were a more sensitive person, but it's enough to make me slip my gun into the waistband of my jeans. Quincy turns back to LaRue. "It's over, honey. But you can trust me. Your secret is safe with me," she repeats, kissing his cheek before standing. She takes a step over to the other man, wrapping her arms around his waist to give him a brief hug. "Take care of him, Spence."

He nods, giving her a small smile as she steps back. "I will,

Quin," he promises, before holding his hand out for LaRue to take. He hauls him up and against his chest, kissing the man's forehead as he rubs his palms up and down his lover's biceps.

Quincy walks over to me, her body angled toward mine as she directs the words at the couple over by the bed. "I'll tell them it was a misunderstanding. We wanted our last week to be an epic getaway just the two of us, to go out with a bang at the end of our one-year contract, and we were having so much fun that we lost track of days."

"Ma'am, there's a video of him forcing you into his car," I tell her.

"Oh that?" She scoffs. "I was being a brat. He wanted to surprise me, but I wanted to know where we were going." She looks at LaRue expectantly, silently asking if he agrees to her story.

He nods. "Thank you, sweet Quincy. I'm very sorry for my panic and distrust. I should've known better," he apologizes in his thick French accent.

"Think nothing of it," she replies, and then she tilts her head back to look up at me. "Ready?"

"Uh… yeah," I agree, and I stand there awkwardly as she gathers her few belongings, shoves them into her giant purse, and hurries into the bathroom to change. When she emerges, she's dressed in jeans and a fitted T-shirt with flip-flops on her feet, and shoves her nightgown into her bag.

As the hotel room door closes behind us, I shake my head at the turn of events, pulling my phone out of my pocket. When

Mrs. Witt answers, I tell her I have Quincy and to send a car to pick her up.

I'm ready for my reward for a job well done.

epilogue

THE METALLIC CLINKING SOUND FILLS the private room of the New York underground BDSM club, as Clarice's naked body is lifted into the air by her ankles. Her sculpted legs are spread by a bar between her feet, leaving her exposed.

I take a deep breath, enjoying the clean scent of the room and the coolness of the air. At my club back home, I have to wear a leather hooded mask at all times to keep my identity hidden. All the Doms do. But when I'm out of town with Clarice, where no one knows me, I get to be free, which means I get to use my mouth on her—my favorite thing in the world.

When she's at the right height, suspended midair, putting her several feet off the ground in order to have her mouth at just the right level, I hit the button to lock the chain in place, leaving her perfectly safe. Her eyes stare into mine heatedly, waiting to see just what I'm going to do to her this time.

As talkative as she is when I'm letting her top me, she's a very well-behaved submissive, staying completely silent and waiting for instruction, making me crave her even more. Such a conundrum. So utterly perfect for me.

I prowl over to her, dropping down on my haunches so we are face-to-face, and then lean forward enough to brush my lips over her upside-down ones. "I'm going to own this pretty little mouth, lover," I murmur there, and I hear her shuddered inhale. "Ah, you like that idea, do you?" I smirk, pulling back enough to look in her eyes.

"Yes, Knight," she breathes, making my cock jerk inside my black jeans at the use of my Dom name. I so rarely get to hear it coming from her that it has an immediate effect, unlike when I'm at my own club, where that's the only name anyone knows me by—besides my partners, of course.

I stay there for a moment, squatted down in front of her, and slide my hand up her trapped nudity. First over her taut nipples, then up her now panting ribs, her soft stomach, then higher to her smooth pubic bone. Finally, I reach up and over the hill of her pussy and dip my finger inside her drenched heat. "Already wet for me. Such a good girl," I tell her, and lean in once more for one last kiss before I stand, looking down into her open slit. It's shining with her arousal, and my erection strains against the denim of my pants, demanding to be free. "Take my cock out, and fill that smart mouth up with as much as you can take," I command.

Like the good little submissive she is, she instantly follows my orders, and my knees almost buckle as the heat of her mouth and throat sucks me inside. Wrapping my arms around the back of her, I grip her ass for a moment. The irresistible feeling of her meaty globes filling my palms and then some makes me thrust into her, making her gag. The sound is intoxicating, and I do it again, pulling back just enough to let her take a breath as I watch her pussy clench. The slight flutter of her opening is enough to have my face diving downward to devour her, and she moans around my cock.

If it were up to her, I'd fuck her throat until she cried, but for some reason, I just can't do it. She'd love for me to be way more deviant, the way I was before I met her, but she's just so small, so fragile-looking next to my over six and half foot build. And I try to ignore the other reasons that may keep me from including too much sadism into our scenes. Right now, I just want to focus on the taste of her delicious juices, and the feel of her smooth, plump folds on my tongue.

Suddenly, I feel her hands clutch the back of my upper thighs to pull herself closer to me, and the insubordination has me instantly reacting. I let go of her with my right hand and slap her ass, my giant hand surely leaving a mark on her naked flesh. She squeals in response, letting go of my legs, which causes her to swing slightly away. Her breaths are coming out in sharp pants, and I glance down to make sure she's all right still in her inverted position. Her face is a mask of pure pleasure, letting me know she's okay, so I bury my face back between her legs.

I eat her like a starved man until she's screaming around my cock, the vibrations of her throat making me want to fuck into her, but I refrain, enjoying the feel of her pussy flexing around my tongue as she comes.

I step away, my swollen shaft leaving her mouth with an audible pop, and I move over to the wall to let her down slowly until her body lies flat on the padded part of the floor face-up. I'd love nothing more than to drag this out, to toy with her for long hours until we can barely move, but I have to have her. Precum already weeps from the head of my dick, and if I don't take her now, a slight breeze will have me coming all over the floor where I stand. So I return to her, unlatching the chains from the bar instead of unbuckling her ankles, forcing her legs to stay open for me, and I flip her over easily, her small yet curvy body feeling as if it weighs nothing.

She groans, the sexy sound filling the room as I pull her up on all fours and put my knees between hers, sliding the crown of my cock up and down her dripping slit. She trembles with anticipation and self-control, remaining completely still even though I know she wants to thrust back to force me deep inside her. So I reward her by feeding her pussy with my steel rod, inch after pulsing inch.

Her elbows buckle as I bump her cervix, so I grip her hips tight until she steadies herself once more. I slide one hand up her long spine and into the back of her hair, making a fist and turning her head to the side so I can watch her profile as I begin to fuck her. Using long, smooth thrusts, I watch her brow furrow and her lips form a silent O as I pull out and dive back in over and over, controlling her movements easily with one hand gripping her thick hair and the other digging into the fleshiness of her womanly hips.

Her moans escalate until she's screaming once again, and this time I follow her over the edge, pumping sharp streams of my hot cum inside her. I fold over her, placing my hands on the floor beside hers so I'm on all fours with her beneath me, spooning her without laying us down to catch our breath.

When we've finally come down from our high, I slide gently out of her, sitting back on my ass as her front half lowers to rest on the floor, giving me a view of her ass and pussy that has my cock stirring back to life immediately. But for right now, I unbuckle the padded shackles around her and massage her ankles, listening to her sweet purr of pleasure.

I stand and scoop her up in my arms, carrying her over to the leather chair against the wall. I sit down and hold her in my lap, holding her like a baby as I run my fingers through her hair, smoothing it back from her perfect face as she sighs contently. When she melts completely into me, I lean down and place soft, sweet kisses to her lips, basking in the rare intimacy she allows me during aftercare.

After a few silent minutes, she's the one who speaks first.

"So what was the real story of the couple in the picture?" Clarice asks, cuddling deeper into my chest.

"What?" I prompt, my mind still fuzzy from the amazing orgasm I just had and the spell she put me under with her closeness.

"The chick you rescued and her kidnapper. What was their real story? Or I guess that is their story—a captive and her kidnapper—which means I was *way* off in Lyra's and my game," she murmurs, sounding disappointed.

"Nah, there was more to it, but I promised I wouldn't tell." I smile mischievously as her face shoots up to glare at me.

"You've gotta be kidding me," she growls. "You can't just tease me like that!"

I chuckle, holding her tighter to my chest. "What was your guess, when you were making up their story as you took their picture?"

Her sparkling eyes dart between mine as she raises a brow. "His facial hair was so freaking perfect, and his eyebrows… those bitches were arched better than mine. They seemed more like Will and Grace than lovers. I guessed she was his beard, a woman pretending to be his girlfriend or wife while he was secretly gay. Either that, or she didn't know he was, because he was setting off my gaydar like crazy."

I throw my head back and laugh, and when I finally come down a little from my amusement, I tell her, "You are one incredible woman, my beautiful lover. You have quite the superpower."

She beams at me. "You mean I was right? I am pretty great at reading people."

I shrug. "I meant your ability to hold my big ass in the palm of your tiny hand. But yeah, that too." And before she can get all weird about my confession of how much she means to me, I kiss her like my life depends on it.

Because really, it does.

The End

Note from the Author

Brian is one of the four main characters in my Club Alias series. They are a group of Doms who own a BDSM club, but are also mercenaries who work tirelessly to clear up bad guys who slip through the judicial system's cracks. Those evil people who escape justice with their loads of money and fancy lawyers—my guys take care of them and make it all look like karma.

To catch up on my Club Alias series, you can find them on Amazon in this reading order:

Before the Lie (Confession Duet Book 1)

Truth Revealed (Confession Duet Book 2)

Seven

You can also find the Confession Duet in a boxed set, both books inside one cover for a special price here.

Coming Soon

Doc

Knight

You will also find Brian in three more upcoming novellas inside other Kindle Worlds!

To keep up with my delicious Doms, follow me on Facebook here, and you can also join my reader group here!

It was such an amazing experience writing in Aleatha's Kindle World! From picking who to link my Brian to, to deciding just how his mission would play out, it was so much fun writing this novella. Thank you so much, Aleatha, for the opportunity. It's definitely surreal going from a hardcore fan for almost five years, to being an author writing a story inside your world.

Thank you, Cassy Roop, as always, for my beautiful cover and formatting. Your talent knows no bounds. Barbara Hoover and Becky Johnson, my favorite editors in all the land, you always make my books so much better than what they started as. And thank you so much, Susan Henn and Victoria Klick, for everything. I couldn't have written this without your insight into the twisted and awesome Fidelity World. Finally, thank you to my Twinnie, Erin Noelle, who let me include one of my favorite characters of hers, Lyra, as my Clarice's photographer friend. You can find her in Erin's EXP1RE and ETERN1TY.

KARMA'S
pawn

prologue

Brian

THE BUZZING ON MY NIGHTSTAND WAKES me from a deep sleep. I open one eye and feel around on the surface until I grasp my phone then squint at the screen before answering. "Williams?"

"Hey, man. Sorry to call so early, but I have a special case for you and it's kinda time sensitive," my old friend tells me, and I pull the phone away from my face to see it's only 3:08 a.m.

"What's happened?" I murmur, clearing my throat and sitting up in bed.

"You remember my sister? She's a doctor there in North Carolina," he prompts.

I wipe my hand down my face, still trying to get my dial tone. "Uh… yeah. Courtney, right?"

"Yeah. She's got a patient right now who came in about two hours ago. She's pretty beat up—the patient I mean. Courtney's having trouble pulling answers out of her, but she did agree to do a rape kit. The questions she *has* answered made Courtney call me, but I'm in the middle of a case here in California myself. So that's why I'm calling you, since you're in the same state as her. She's only about an hour away from you. You're still in Fayettenam, right?"

"I am," I reply, throwing the covers off me and standing.

"And you're still in the business of... taking care of people, right? Secure line, so you can answer freely."

"Yep. If the fucker fits our code—life for a life—karma tags me in," I tell him, making sure he remembers my mercenary team doesn't kill just anyone. They have to deserve it. The assholes who escape justice with their big bank accounts and slimeball lawyers.

"Brian, from the sound of it, this guy fits the bill... multiple times over." His voice goes deep with the last part, and the hair on my arms prickle.

I pull on my jeans and slide my feet into my boots, reaching for a shirt. "I'm on it. What's the address?"

chapter 1

Brian

"DON'T TELL ME," CLARICE ANSWERS on the third ring, her sleepy voice making me smile.

"Another mission, lover," I sigh into the phone. "This one in Raleigh."

I hear her move in bed, the covers probably finding their way between her knees like she prefers—one leg in, one leg out. "Well, at least there's that. I just so happen to be in Raleigh right now, shooting a *bridal extravaganza*," she says, the last words coming out in a deepened dramatic voice like a game show prize announcer.

I chuckle. "You think you could stand keeping me company after just seeing me in New York?"

"Bri, I can always stand keeping you company. Silly question.

I've got a hotel room already, so save the per diem and buy me something pretty," she orders, and my dick twitches, even though I know she's joking. I love it when she gets bossy.

"Yes, mistress," I tell her, making her giggle.

"I'll text you the hotel details. When will you be here?" she asks.

"In about half an hour. I'm on the road now." I turn on my blinker, taking the I-40 exit heading to the state capital, my heart beating rapidly now that I know I'll get to see my Clarice.

Not yours.

I shake off the aggravating voice, listening to Clarice stretch on the other end of the line.

"Okay, texting you now. I'm savoring my last thirty minutes of sleep," she tells me.

I growl, suddenly remembering I won't see her right away. "You'll get more than that. I have to talk to a vic who's in the hospital before I can head to you. Plus, I know you'll want details, and I don't have any yet. So text me and go back to sleep, beautiful. I'll wake you up."

"Yes, Daddy," she murmurs, and I stifle a groan. "See you in a bit."

We hang up, and not a minute later, I receive the address to the hotel that's not very far away from Courtney's hospital. Thank God. It's getting harder and harder to go any length of time without seeing Clarice. She's more than just a friend with benefits. She's been my best friend since we met when I was deployed to Afghanistan years ago, while she was there taking photographs for a magazine. She meets up with me whenever I'm on a mission for my mercenary team, which is disguised behind a legitimate security company. I'm also co-owner of a BDSM club my teammates and I run. I wasn't really into the lifestyle before becoming part of the four of us who own the place, but after learning so much about it, and many therapy sessions with our leader, Doc—the company's resident psychologist who created our mercenary team—I found I was way more into it than I first believed.

But unlike Corbin, Seth, and Doc, who are all exclusively Dominants as far as I know, I'm what's called a switch. I mostly identify as a Dom, but there's just something about Clarice taking control that satisfies me in a way that's far more than sexual. I feel free, like I'm soaring, whenever I give in to her and let her top me. And even better, I'm sure it does something for her, having so much control over such a giant of a man. She's more than a foot shorter than my six foot eight frame, yet she can bring me to my knees, making her tower over me—and my heart.

But right now, I need to focus on the mission.

———

AFTER RECEIVING A visitor's badge from the nurse at the front desk, I hurry down the corridor of the emergency room, my eyes scanning the whole way. Passing by another nurses station, I see a short, feminine, dark-haired figure in a white doctor's coat step out of a curtained-off cubicle and wave at me, waiting for me to approach.

"Hey, Brian. Thank you for coming. My brother said you could help far better than he can from California," she tells me, a mix of gratefulness and worry marring her pretty face. She looks just like a female version of Williams, with her almost perfect features. Not my type though.

Focus.

"No problem. What do we know so far?"

She takes hold of my arm and tugs me away from the curtain, speaking in a low tone. "She was most definitely sexually assaulted. I haven't been able to pull much out of her, but she keeps repeating something. 'He'll kill me too.' Over and over again. She's got strangulation marks around her neck that indicate he was using some type of twine or wire. A policeman found her in the park during his routine check, and we think her attacker heard him coming and got away. Interrupted just in time. He was able to give her CPR when he felt a faint pulse."

"Fuck," I hiss. "Okay, can I go in there and ask her a few questions?"

"If she's still awake. She's been in and out of consciousness since she got here," Courtney replies, and I nod, turning to head into the curtained room.

When I walk in, the sight before me makes me flinch. It's one thing seeing photos and graphic police reports of victims when

I'm handed another mission. But it's another thing entirely seeing it in person.

Doc formed our mercenary group several years ago after hearing his sexual assault patients' stories and not being able to do anything about the fuckers who got away with what they did to them. Finally, he decided enough was enough, approaching and hiring me right as I got out of the military. I've been on a countless number of missions now, acting as karma's pawn and doling out justice, making it all look like an accident.

But unlike most of the people in the files I'm given, this girl is miraculously alive. She can't be more than eighteen, and she looks half dead with all her bruises, cuts, and swelling. The line around the front of her throat is so brutal it's hard to look at.

Her eyes open slightly, sensing someone in the room with her, so I soften my features and speak gently. "I'm Brian. I'm here to ask you a few questions about what happened. Is that okay?"

She looks me up and down, trying to read me, not knowing whether to trust me or not. I sit on the chair next to her bed, positioning me eye level with her so she doesn't have to look up at me, putting her somewhat at ease, but worry fills her face.

"He'll kill me too," she whispers, her voice sounding painfully scratchy.

"What's your name, sweetheart?" I ask, keeping my voice calm.

"T-Tabitha."

"Tabitha, can you tell me anything about the person who did this to you?"

She shakes her head and gasps with pain. "No. He'll kill me too." The panic enters her tone, and the monitors next to the bed begin to beep.

"Shhh, it's okay. I've got a secret. But you have to promise not to tell. You swear?" I prompt, looking into her youthful eyes.

She struggles to fight back her fear, and answers meekly, "I swear."

"I'm very, very good at finding bad guys. It's my job, and I will not let him hurt you again."

"Are… are you a cop?" she whispers.

"No, not exactly. I have a security company, so I'll be able to protect you. I just need you to give me something to go on," I urge, trying my best to send her good vibes so she'll feel I'm someone she can trust.

She blinks. "That's good. The cops can't help. He said they tried before, but he didn't get in trouble."

"Can you tell me what happened to you? Anything you can remember will help. Even the tiniest detail."

"There… there were three of us there. I was going back to my college campus after leaving the coffee shop. The next thing I remember, I woke up in some strange house. None of us knew where we were or how we got there. I think that was three days ago. I'm not sure though, because he kept us somewhere with no windows. The first day, he took the girl named Christina. He never brought her back. Some time passed, not sure how long, but I think it was only a day. That's when he took Susan. Again, she didn't come back. Then last night, he came and got me. He took me to a park and started choking me. He… he…."

Seeing her eyes well up with tears, I reach out my hand, palm up, offering for her to take it. She tentatively does, her fingers icy inside my hot hand as my blood pressure starts to rise at the images she's painting.

"He raped me, and while he was doing it, he took a piece of silver… like, wire stuff, and wrapped it around my throat until I couldn't breathe. I thought I was going to die. Everything went black and I thought I was dead. But then I felt something heavy on my chest, someone shaking me, rocking my whole body, and it hurt so bad I took a deep breath and tried to scream. Which made me realize I wasn't dead after all. But knowing what he'd just done to me, and how bad everything hurts, it might've been better if I had." She sobs, her tears spilling over, and I reach to the stand behind me, grabbing some tissues to hand to her.

"Never, Tabitha. You will get through this. Trust me. I know the best therapist on the entire planet, and he's only an hour away from here. If anyone can help you heal from this, it's Doc," I implore, squeezing her fingers gently.

"We all stayed at school during a weeklong break. No one probably even realizes we were missing. No one knows they're—" Another sob.

I shush her once more, enclosing her tiny hand between both of mine. "Don't worry about that. I'll let the police know, and they'll take care of that part. We're just focusing on catching the bad guy, okay? That way he'll never have a chance to hurt anyone else."

"But the police will just let him go again," she whimpers.

"No, sweetheart. You don't understand. Remember that secret you promised to keep?" I wait for her nod. "Once I find this guy, the police won't have a chance to fuck up again." I let my words hang in the air, and after a few moments, I see one side of her lips quirk.

"Security company you said?" she whispers.

I wink. "Or something like that."

chapter 2

Brian

THE HOTEL ROOM DOOR OPENS RIGHT as I lift my hand to knock, and I'm greeted by the most beautiful sight known to man—a naked Clarice. But even as I devour her with my hungry stare, I step forward to fill the doorway with my hulking frame, ensuring no one could possibly peek at an image that would get them killed before they even processed what they were seeing.

"What if I was a maid?" I growl, tossing my bag down just inside the room.

"Too early for housekeeping, big guy," she purrs as she takes a step back. Her sultry voice combined with her pet name for me, along with her glorious nudity, makes me painfully erect behind my zipper.

I step inside and shut the door behind me, putting the latch in place, before leaning back against it. My eyes trail over her intoxicating features, from the top of her dark, sleep-ruffled hair, to the tips of her light-pink painted toenails. And everything in between makes my heart pound inside my chest like I've been racing around like Jason Statham in *Crank*.

I have gone to war for my country, held the line when we confronted our enemies. I have faced some of the evilest creatures ever spawned, unworthy of even being called human beings. I have taken countless lives, all in the name of justice. Yet none of that compares to the surge of pure adrenalin that enters my bloodstream when all I do is lay eyes on a tiny woman named Clarice.

My control breaks, and I surge forward, picking her up and slamming my mouth down on hers all in one swift move that lands us dead center on the king-size bed. Her throaty chuckle as she takes a breath makes me thrust unconsciously, and I grind into her heat. She stills suddenly, and I pull back far enough to look into her beautiful face.

"You know the rules." She quirks an eyebrow at me. "Not until your mission is complete. Until then, I'm in control."

I force my body to relax, taking calming breaths. She's right. Those are our rule. I spin us until she's on top of me, and the view of her luscious tits hovering above me soothes any discouragement I might've felt. She pulls her knees up my sides until she's straddling my stomach, and I feel her wet inferno against my abs, making me groan.

"Now, be a good boy and tell me about the job you're on," she says, skimming her hands beneath my tee, pushing it up to my armpits before leaning forward and trailing breathy kisses over my chest.

"Seems there's a killer on the loose," I rumble, my hips twitching upward slightly when she licks across my nipple, but I take control over my own body, reminding it that if I move, she'll stop. Completely. And won't let me touch her again for a full day. The little minx. She loves to torment me.

"Ooo, sounds dangerous." She slides her nose up my sternum, breathing me in. The look on her face does torturous things to my heart, closing her eyes and smiling gently, like my scent is comforting her. Hers does the same to me.

"My job is always dangerous, lover." I catch the look of worry flash across her delicate features before she hides it. "But you know I'm invincible." It's something I tell her every time we talk about my work. We both know it's not true, but we also know I'm damn good at my job, and I wouldn't let *anything* take me away from her. She's my reason to breathe, whether she acknowledges it or not.

"Details, big guy. Give them to me," she whispers over my chest, tickling across the light hair there.

"Rape victim survived being strangled nearly to death in a park. Said she was one of three girls who were being held captive. The other two never came back after the perp took them one by one. Police interrupted and he ran off. I got some details I need to discuss with Seth, see if he can dig for any more info," I ground out, and then sigh in relief when she reaches for the button and fly of my jeans.

"Is this a pro bono job?" she whispers down the middle of my stomach.

"Favor for an old friend."

She grasps hold of my open jeans and yanks them off my hips and down my legs, my erection standing at attention. "What old friend?" Clarice asks, and for a brief moment, I think I detect a hint of jealousy in her tone.

"Buddy from the army. He stayed in when I got out, and let's just say, he's pretty high ranking now. The type of guy who'd drop everything if you needed him, and this time he needed me. The New York job paid really well, so I'm not worried about making any money right now."

She grasps hold of my cock and breathes over the tip. "For such a big, tough man, you have such a good, soft heart, Bri."

The heart she mentioned soars at her praise, and I glance down at her, still holding perfectly still, even though all I want to do is thrust upward into her hot, waiting mouth. "There's nothing soft about me, lover," I tell her, moving my eyes from hers to my proud shaft and back again, and she giggles. "Soft, no. Loyal, yes. There's nothing I wouldn't do for you and my friends."

She lifts an eyebrow. "Me and your friends? Why am I separate in that statement? Aren't I your friend?"

"You're separate, because you're on a-whole-nother level. You—"

Before I can convey how much she means to me, she cuts off my words by swallowing my cock, and I nearly go cross-eyed as I groan to the ceiling. Such a Clarice thing to do. She never lets me get too deep in conversations dealing with us, so I was surprised by her questions to begin with. Am I finally making my way into her heart the way she buried herself inside mine all those years ago? All I can do is continue to show her what she means to me, until she'll let me tell her with my words. Words she never wants to hear.

chapter 3

Brian

"WHAT'S UP, BRO? WE STILL ON for tonight?" Seth, one of my partners at the security company and BDSM club, asks over the phone the next morning.

"Sorry, I had to leave town in the middle of the night. Job in Raleigh for a friend. Mind helping me out?" I ask, knowing he's got plenty of work to do. But he's the computer guru, the technological genius of the team, and we couldn't complete any of our missions without his brain and skills.

"No problem. I just finished helping Doc out with something, and I have about half an hour before I'm supposed to meet Twyla for lunch."

"Should be plenty of time. You at your spaceship?" I question, referring to his hulking computer setup. The guy graduated in his teens from MIT. I couldn't tell you half the shit he's got hooked up to that thing, just that it has three giant monitors that practically surround him when he sits in the neon green leather chair he's got parked in the center.

"Always," he replies, and I hear him type something in.

"Okay, here's what's going on. Three girls were kidnapped at different times just outside their college campus almost a week ago. Two are missing, presumed dead, and the third was found in a park after the perp was interrupted while he was strangling her, after he sexually assaulted her." I give him the CliffsNotes then continue with what Tabitha told me before I left the hospital. "These aren't the first girls who have gone missing. It's all been kept hush-hush around the school, so much so that Tabitha admitted she thought it was just rumors. And the chancellor chalks it up to them quitting college and running off."

"How have they kept it hush-hush? Haven't the missing girls' families been freaking out and searching for them?" Seth asks, and I hear him typing again. "Nothing on the Internet about missing college girls in Raleigh in the past year."

"That's the thing. The three girls had no families. They're going to school on scholarships and were foster kids. Being eighteen to twenty years old, they're adults. I'm thinking if you could look into people there on scholarships, and cross-reference them with people who have gone AWOL, we'd find a couple girls who fit the same MO. No one would've come looking for them," I explain.

"On it," Seth assures. "So this guy is pretty smart then. Choosing victims who wouldn't cause an uproar. And he has the ability to look into their records, to know who they are. How?"

"Another thing, Tabitha, the survivor, told me, 'The cops can't help. He said they tried before, but he didn't get in trouble.' Is there any way to look up police reports that didn't pan out, maybe? Something got this asshole on their radar at some point, but they didn't find anything to convict him. Which means he also must keep the girls somewhere other than where he lives if the cops didn't discover anything that arose suspicion."

"That'll take me a little while, but I'll see if anything links up. Give me a bit and I'll call you back," he tells me.

"Thanks, man."

After we hang up, I fall back against the mattress in the hotel room, making Clarice bounce where she's scrolling through photos she took at the event yesterday. "When you gotta leave for day two, lover?" I ask.

"The doors open at 11:00 a.m., but I don't need to be there until the wedding dress fashion show at one," she murmurs, using her touchpad to edit the dimness and tone of a picture she took of a massive wedding cake.

I lean close to her, kissing the buttery-soft skin of her shoulder as I watch her work. I love times like these, when it's just the two of us, hanging out and doing mundane, ordinary things. I could spend hours in her silent presence and be completely content. Since the day I met her, we've never had an awkward moment.

It's always a sense of calm that washes over me, as long as we're breathing the same air. It's not until we're back to miles apart when I become my usual aloof self. I try not to be a dick, but it's hard when all I can think about is Clarice and the next time I'll get to see her.

"Oh, check this one out," she says, excitement creeping into her quiet voice.

"What is that?" I ask, squinting and leaning forward a bit to get a closer look.

"It's a cake topper. The bride is squeezing the groom's butt," she giggles, and I shake my head.

"Would someone actually put that on their wedding cake?" I ask, chuckling.

"I think it's cute. It'd have to be a pretty badass couple with a great sense of humor to pull it off. I personally like this one," she says, and when she zooms in, I can't help but throw my head back and laugh.

"Now that's some funny shit right there," I agree, eyeing the little statue atop a huge white cake. It's a bride dragging a sitting groom backward by his collar, looking like she's hauling him to the altar.

Just as she's flipping to the next photo, my cell rings. I answer it quickly when I see it's Seth. "What ya got?"

"Okay, I've got a list of eight people. Scholarship awardees who were dropped from their classes by their professors because of unexcused absences. I also have a few police records for you to check out. I'm not sure if they'll be related or not, seeing how no one reported the girls missing that we know of," he explains.

"Perfect. Send them to me. I'll check everything out today," I reply, and I hear my e-mail notification tone go off in my ear.

"Sent."

"Thanks again," I tell Seth.

"No problem, bro. Be careful out there. Something's off about this. I'm going to keep digging to see what I find. Let me know of any new developments."

"Will do. Now go eat with your girl." I pull the cell from my face and bring up the e-mail he just sent me. The first attachment is the records of eight students. I open the nightstand drawer next to me, hoping there's a notepad and pen there, but the only thing in it is a Bible. "Hey, beautiful. Check in your nightstand. I need paper and a pen."

She leans way over, and I hold her thigh so she doesn't fall off the bed, trying to ignore the way her supple flesh fills my hand. "Here you go, big guy. Anything interesting?" she asks, handing me the paper with the hotel's emblem across the top, and a pen with the same graphic in gold.

I begin flipping through the records, jotting down the names of the eight students as I go. When I've got them all written down, I tell her, "Okay, these kids here were going to school on scholarships. They were dropped from their classes because they stopped coming. Totally AWOL. We don't have much to go on right now, but at least we have somewhere to start."

"Well that's good news. What is this list here?" she asks, pointing to the second attachment at the bottom of the e-mail.

"These are police reports Seth said I needed to look into. Hopefully one of them will be from when the killer was questioned and then released," I explain.

And with that, I begin my game of elimination.

FIVE HOURS LATER, I'm completely irritated. Nothing is panning out. With a little bit of research on Google and Facebook, all but two of the people on the list were easy to find. I got excited for a moment, when one of the police reports linked up with one of the other girls' names I couldn't find on the Internet, but was disappointed once more when it was just for a noise violation at some party she was throwing. Further digging showed she'd probably quit school because she'd rather drink and do massive amounts of drugs from the photos on her friends' profiles. She didn't have a Facebook page, but her friends mentioned her name in the captions of their pictures.

The last girl on the list was a ghost. I texted Seth, telling him she was our last hope using that line of thinking, so he's doing his tech-genius thing as I finally stop long enough to feed myself.

My phone rings just as I'm sitting down to eat my sub at Jersey Mike's, and I smile, seeing it's Clarice. "Hello, lover," I answer.

"Any news?" she asks. "Give me something good. I'm bored out of my ever-loving mind. I swear if I ever get married, I'm eloping."

Heat crawls up the back of my neck at the thought of Clarice ever marrying anyone but me. But then I shake myself out of it, knowing I'd take out anyone before they could even get close to her.

"Fucking nada. Everyone on the list but one is accounted for. Seth is digging into her background as we speak. Nothing from the police reports either. I'm completely fucking stumped," I growl into the phone.

"Hey, it's okay, big guy," she soothes, but it doesn't do much to calm my nerves.

I speak quietly. "No, it's not. I'm not used to this shit. Usually, I have a file with all the information I need right there for me. The enemy's location is in black and white. All I gotta do is get in, take care of them, and get out." I lower my voice further. "I'm a mercenary. Not a goddamn detective. I'm… I don't have the capacity to figure this shit out."

"Stop right there, Brian Glover. Not another word in that direction. You are the bravest, most badass, and smartest motherfucker I've ever known—"

"You've never met Seth," I insert.

She growls at my insolence. "Not the point, Bri! I was there with you in New York. You figured it out. You saved that woman."

"Only because of a lucky sh—"

"Zzzzzzz!" She silences me, using Chris Tucker's technique in our favorite movie, *The Fifth Element*. I can't help but chuckle.

She's just so damn cute, especially when she's aggravated with me. "You, big guy, are perfection. You've got this. You'll figure it out and you will save the day once again. You're a goddamn superhero."

I let her words fill me up and overflow as it warms me from head to toe. I take a deep breath, trying to commit what she just told me to memory so I can play it on repeat in my mind for the rest of my damn life.

"Now, calm your tits and tell me, what next?" she prompts, and I do as she says, clearing my mind and trying to think of another avenue of finding this motherfucker.

"Well, Tabitha was pretty out of it when I talked to her last night. Maybe she's had time to recover a bit, at least enough to answer more questions or give me more info of what she remembers," I tell her, hearing what sounds like a car door closing on her end of the line.

"I have an idea. Humor me," she says, and I run my hand through my hair, sliding down farther in my seat.

"Hit me, lover."

"Later," she replies, and even though I know she's joking, my cock twitches inside my pants. "Let me talk to Tabitha." I begin to tell her no, but she cuts me off. "Wait, wait, wait. Hear me out. Bri, you are a giant, hulking, ridiculously handsome man."

"Thank you."

"You're welcome, but I'm not done. But mainly, you are a *man*. That poor girl was just raped and almost murdered by a man after being kidnapped and held hostage by him. She may just talk to me, a woman, more openly than she would a *giant, hulking, ridiculously handsome man* such as yourself," she emphasizes.

I pause, thinking this through. As much as I want to keep Clarice as far away from my actual job while at the same time keeping her as close to me as possible, she's got a point. Finally, I give her the answer she obviously wants to hear. "Okay, I'll text you the hospital info and where to find her. I'll let Courtney know you're coming. Are you finished with your event?"

"Hold up. Who the fuck is Courtney?" she growls, and my brow lifts at her tone.

"Is that jealousy I hear in that sexy voice of yours, lover?" I speak low into the phone, my voice deep and filled with promise.

She clears her throat. "Of course not. I've just never heard of a guy named Courtney before, and you said this job was for your old army buddy, who you most definitely called a he," she flounders.

I chuckle, letting her off the hook. "Courtney is my friend's sister. She's a doctor at the hospital where Tabitha is. She's the one who called her brother, Williams, about the case, but since he lives in California and is on his own mission at the moment, he called me, knowing I'm close. Also, she's married. And you're way hotter, my beautiful Clarice," I add, hearing her sigh.

"That's acceptable. Okay, text me the shit. And then let me know what Seth says about the last chick on the list," she orders, making me smile.

"Yes, ma'am. I hope you're enjoying all this bossiness, but just so you know, when it's my turn, you're in for it," I warn, and I take in the sultry sound of her laugh.

"I look forward to it."

chapter 4

Clarice

"Courtney?" I prompt, walking up to the doctor who fits the description Brian gave me of his friend's sister.

"Yes. Clarice, right? Brian told me you were on your way. Thank you for coming." She reaches out and we shake hands. "I really think she may open up to you more than she has been with the police. She's talked to me a lot, but nothing of importance. I've tried to distract her when she's awake, to keep her mind off what she just went through," she says, looking a bit frazzled.

"Is everything all right?" I ask, taking in the way she keeps looking up and down the hallway and glancing at her clipboard.

Her eyes turn to me. "Oh, yes, yes. Sorry. Just a bit overwhelmed at the moment. With this flu epidemic, there are several doctors and nurses out and we're low on staff. But don't worry about me. Tabitha is right in there. Go on in and good luck," she tells me, reaching out to touch my arm warmly before hurrying off.

I take a few steps until I'm just outside the private room Courtney had pointed me to. I knock on the door lightly before moving inside, watching the girl's head turn toward me. And it breaks my heart the moment my eyes land on her bruised and swollen face.

"Tabitha? Hi, my name is Clarice. My friend Brian came to see you last night. Do you remember him?" I ask gently. She swallows thickly, and that's when I see her throat. An image of the way those marks could've gotten there flashes through my mind, and I shiver.

"Super-duper tall?" she murmurs.

"Yes, that's him." I smile, taking a few steps closer.

She lifts her hand to push back her hair, and I see it's all taped up with an IV inserted. "He was really nice. I've talked to a lot of people today, but he was the nicest," she informs.

I nod, my face softening. "Yeah, he's pretty amazing. Do you mind if I sit and chat with you a while?"

She seems to think about it for moment, but then eventually nods toward the chair next to her bed.

Knowing Brian is waiting for any new information I can pull out of her, I don't waste any time with small talk. But I start with an assurance, so she doesn't get frustrated having to repeat herself to yet another person. "Brian told me everything you could remember, but I just wanted to see, since you've gotten some rest, if maybe you recalled anything since you spoke to him."

Her eyes lower, like she's ashamed she can't be of more help. "No, not really. I told the police everything I remembered too. Told them how he said they let him go last time. They just promised they wouldn't this time if they caught him. But I don't believe them."

"Can you elaborate on that a little for me? Did he say anything more about the police letting him go? Like maybe, why they questioned him in the first place? Any little detail could really be helpful, even if you think it's something insignificant." I scoot closer, placing my arm along the bed rail, and then resting my chin on my fist.

She thinks on this for a while, closing her eyes. She leans her head back against the bed, her brow furrowing. "I'm trying to remember his exact words. He kept saying, 'They caught me before, but they let me go. They'll just let me go again.' And another time, he said, 'They knew I did it, but they didn't care. They still set me free.' He was... weird. Like, scary weird. Even before he came and took the other girls out of the place he was keeping us."

"What scared you about him? Was he scary-*looking*? Was his voice frightening?"

"No, no. Nothing like that. I mean, the fact we couldn't see what he looked like was pretty terrifying. He wore this... mask thing. It was a clear plastic mask, but you still couldn't see what he looked like. It distorted his face enough you couldn't make out his features. And he wore a beanie, so I don't know what color his hair was. The only thing I could tell is I think he was white. Through the clear mask, I could see he wasn't dark-skinned. His hands too."

I nod, making a mental note to tell Brian all these new details. "What about the girls? Did you know the others before it happened? You all went to the same school."

She shakes her head gently. "I didn't *know* them, know them. But we're all in the same…" She trails off, her eyes misting over.

Without thinking, I reach out and take her hand, careful not to disturb her IV. Surprisingly, her grip tightens around mine. "You're all in the same what, Tabitha?" I urge her to continue.

A lone tear escapes and travels down her bruised cheek. "Nothing. We aren't all in the same anything anymore. Because they're dead. They're both dead. I know they are, because he didn't bring them back. And if he did to them what he did to me, then—"

I interrupt her, watching her blood pressure rise the longer she speaks. "Hey, it's okay. It's okay." She closes her eyes, visibly fighting for strength, and when she opens them a minute later, I ask her once more, "Where did you know them from before?"

Her voice is quieter when she replies, "We were in an after-school group together. Like a support group. One for former foster kids. I had only recently started going. Been maybe three or four times. So I didn't really know anyone yet. I'm a freshman, and they were sophomores."

"That's good, Tabitha. Very good." I squeeze her hand.

"There were rumors… that two other girls from the group had gone missing before I joined. But people kept saying they just dropped out without disenrolling. And how would anyone know? They didn't have any family. And the friends they had made at school went ignored, even when some of them said the girls never said anything about quitting. One was a junior. Why would she drop out just a year from graduating? But the chancellor always just shot it down."

"This chancellor is really starting to get on my nerves," I grumble.

"Chancellor Montgomery? He's actually really nice. I think he wants to just keep everything on the down low, since we're supposedly the safest campus in the state. I wouldn't want anything to mess with that title either, if I didn't know for a fact what was really going on. But now we do. And as soon as everyone comes back from break, they'll finally know the truth." Her jaw clenches, and that little bit of defiance lets me know that Tabitha will eventually be just fine. She's a fighter.

But then what she said makes me question, "Back from break?"

"Yeah, we're in the middle of spring break right now. The other girls and I had stayed behind, because, well… we had nowhere else to go. We don't have any family to visit during break, so we all stayed in the dorms.

"We had set up two group meetings this week instead of just the one, just to make sure all of us were handling the downtime alone all right. It was after our Monday meeting when he…

grabbed me. Christina and Susan weren't there at the meetup, but we all just assumed they found friends to go home with, or decided to go to the beach. Now I know—he had already taken them. Because they were there when he threw me in with them."

Something niggles at the back of my mind, telling me this is the missing information we've been waiting for. With none of Brian's original searches panning out, I follow this line of thinking. "Tabitha, when is the next meet-up supposed to be?

"Friday at 6:00 p.m.," she replies, and I glance at my Apple Watch then lift my eyes to hers. She must see the wheels in my mind turning, because she asks timidly, "Do... do you think he's going to do it again?"

I give her a reassuring smile. "Hopefully almost getting caught will have deterred him."

"What day is it today? I... I kind of lost track of time when he had us. It was always dark in there."

"It's Friday, honey," I reply, my throat clogging with emotion thinking about what this poor thing must have been through.

"The police didn't question me about the other girls at all. Just about *him*. They... they have no idea we were in the group together, that there were other missing girls from before."

I let go of her hand and pat her leg before leaning back in the chair, preparing to stand. "It's okay. I can let them know what you said, and they'll probably want to come get this new information from y—"

"No, don't tell them. They'll just let him go again. It has to be

Brian. Brian promised he'd take care of everything and not let the police mess up again." Her eyes are pleading.

"All right, honey. That's what I'll do then. You rest up, and I'll call Brian."

A few minutes later, after I buckle myself into my car, I grab my cell out of my bag and hurriedly call Brian. It goes straight to voice mail, so I leave him a message. "Hey, Bri. I just left the hospital. I have a hunch. Tabitha said she knew the other girls she was trapped with from a support group for foster kids. Their next meeting is this evening in about twenty minutes at Hartensteiner Coffee. I'm gonna go and see if any of the other members might've seen anything suspicious."

I toss my phone back in my purse and back out of the parking spot. I know exactly where the coffee shop is that the meeting is taking place, because it's right next to the convention center where the bridal show I've been shooting is located. It sends a chill up my spine when I realize the coffee shop is within walking distance of the school these girls are being taken from and the event I've been working. I've never been so close to something so horrible happening *right now*. It's an eerie feeling, like someone is watching you, plotting to make you the next victim. Much different from visiting sites where terrible events took place in the past. This isn't a history lesson. This will be one in the future. Documentaries will be made about this new Campus Killer. His name will be mentioned alongside Ted Bundy, BTK, and Jeffrey Dahmer.

"Yeah, and here your crazy ass goes snooping around for clues while he's still out there," I mumble to myself, shaking my head. But I have to help Brian. I can't let him go around thinking he's not smart enough to solve this. He's the most heroic person I know, a real-life superhero in my eyes. I have to do whatever I can to help him stop this fucker.

I pull into the small parking lot of the coffee shop and back into a spot. Shutting down the engine, I take a deep breath and let it out to calm my nerves before grabbing my bag and heading inside.

The place is dimly lit, and as I glance farther inside, I see there are booths with individual lamps on each table. The coffee counter is to the far left, with a stage at the very back of the space. It has almost an English pub feel to it, with its dark wood everything, and if I didn't know this was the hunting ground for a serial killer, I'd become a regular because of its atmosphere alone.

Just inside the door, on the wall to my right, there is a bulletin board. Fliers for different events, open mic nights, and groups are pinned all over it, overlapping and curling at the edges. A bunch have phone number tabs at the bottom to rip off and take with you, and it's between a few missing tabs that I spot one word in bold black letters printed on blue paper: *Foster.*

I pull out some of the pins and rearrange them on the bulletin board until I can fully read the one I unbury.

FFKNCS
Former Foster Kids of NC State

Meetups Weekly
at Hartensteiner Coffee
Fridays at 6:00 p.m.
All are welcome.

Suddenly, I realize there's no guarantee these people will be willing to talk to me. With the chancellor in their ear telling them they have nothing to worry about, the rumors aren't true, then they're probably not open to discussing things for fear they'll get into trouble.

I pull down the FFKNCS flier and stuff it into my bag, deciding I'll pretend to be a new student. I can easily pass as one in my high ponytail, skinny jeans, simple T-shirt, and Converse. I'd dressed for comfort today, knowing I'd be walking around the convention center for hours. That sounded more likely to get answers to my questions after the meeting, instead of freaking them out with "I'm searching for clues to stop a serial killer targeting your group."

I walk farther into the coffee shop, looking around to see if I can spot anyone who might be waiting for a meeting to begin. Most of the tables taken up are occupied by couples, sets of people with their books open along with their laptops. It's not very crowded—not surprising since it's spring break. Finally, I spot a round table near the stage at the back of the shop. No one has anything out, not a computer or book in sight, and I have a feeling this is the group I'm looking for.

Heading toward them, I wait until I'm close and then pull out the flier, hoping they see me getting it out of my bag and will think I've had it a while instead of just having swiped it from the board. When I approach, I hike my purse up higher on my shoulder and greet them with a warm smile.

"Hi there. Is this FFK support group? My name is Clar—" I clear my throat, rethinking giving them my real name. "Excuse me. Claire. I just moved here from out of state, and someone on campus gave me this." I hold out the flier.

A young man, maybe twenty-three, in black-rimmed glasses stands and holds out his hand. "Yes, that's us. Nice to meet you, Claire. I'm Ciprian. Welcome to the group," he tells me, and I shake his hand before circling the table and taking a seat between a guy and girl, who both look like they're freshmen; so freaking young. And it hurts my heart knowing there is someone out there raping and killing these kids.

"Thank you. And cool name. I wasn't sure if you'd be meeting tonight since the campus is like a ghost town. I'm starting in the mini-semester that begins next week," I tell them, hoping that's still a thing. It's been a long time since I was in college, almost ten years.

"Ah, you're brave," Ciprian says, his eyes twinkling behind his glasses in the dim lighting. "They pack so much information into such a short time. I don't see how y'all can handle those mini-mesters."

I smile, trying to think of what to say next, but I'm thankfully saved from having to speak again when a blonde girl hurries up to the table, hooking her bag onto the back of a chair before plopping into it. "Sorry, guys," she tells everyone, out of breath. "I was waiting around to see if Christina was back so we could walk together, but she still must be off on her adventure. Can't believe that ho went somewhere with Susan and didn't invite me." She huffs, crossing her arms over her chest.

My gut clenches, recognizing the names of the girls Tabitha said she was being held with. These people, their friends, they have no idea anything has happened to them, just assuming they'd gone somewhere for their break from school. They have no clue two are presumed dead and one is in the hospital after narrowly escaping the same fate.

They also have no idea one of them could be next.

chapter 5

Brian

"HEY, BRI. I JUST LEFT THE HOSPITAL. I have a hunch. Tabitha said she knew the other girls she was trapped with from a support group for foster kids. Their next meeting is this evening in about twenty minutes at Hartensteiner Coffee. I'm gonna go and see if any of the other members might've seen anything suspicious."

I exit out of my voice mail and immediately call Clarice back, my blood pressure rising. She must've called while I was trying to dial her at the same time for an update. It rings and rings before her voice mail picks up once more. "Clarice. Don't you dare go there by yourself. There is a goddamn killer on the loose. Go straight to the hotel." I hang up, knowing full well she's already on her way to the coffee shop, if not already there. God knows when she'll get the damn message. So I do a U-turn at the next light and head in that direction.

My phone rings and I look down, hoping it's Clarice. But it's not. "Hey, man. Give me some good news." I answer Seth's call, crossing my fingers that something—anything—turned up from the last girl's name on the list. If not, then I've got to start all the way at the beginning on a different search path.

His voice comes over my car's speakers. "Dude. Wait till you hear this shit," he tells me, and my hackles immediately rise. "Finally found the last girl on the list, Tara. Turns out, she went missing *years* ago, around the same time as another woman, Holly, who was found raped and strangled to death. Her name popped up in several articles with Holly's investigation, conspiring that Tara was also a victim of the same murderer. Nine years ago, he was caught. It was a fucking thirteen-year-old kid who killed Holly."

My head jerks back. "The fuck?"

"Yeah. Can we say 'mommy issues'? Being so young, he was tried as a juvenile and pronounced insane. I didn't have time to delve into everything, but what little I read about this guy in his court report, he was fucking batshit. Anyway, so five years go by, and he's so well behaved and is able to convince the doctors he's been rehabilitated that they let the motherfucker go on his eighteenth birthday."

"That's what she meant," I murmur.

"What?" Seth prompts.

"Tabitha. She told me that he kept bragging the police let

him go. We thought she meant the police came by recently and questioned him, and then didn't find anything to arrest him. No. What he meant is they caught him, and then literally let him go years later. And in his head, he's convinced himself, and also his victims, that if he gets caught, they'll just release him again." My hands tighten on the steering wheel, knowing my Clarice is there in this psychopath's hunting grounds.

"I have a picture of him I'm sending you now. Oh! So, you know how serial killers always have an MO, like the way they kill, who they kill, etcetera? It's usually because in their mind, they are murdering the same person over and over again. Either to get the same feeling they did the first time they did it, or in order to feel what it would be like to kill someone they haven't had the balls to face yet. Comparing all the missing girls—Tara, Christina, and Susan—along with Tabitha and Holly, this guy is targeting women around five and a half feet with long dark hair and no parents. The original victim, Holly, was his foster sister. His parents took her in when she was sixteen. Apparently, he didn't take too kindly to not being an only child anymore."

My phone dings, and I grab it out of my lap to pull up the photo Seth just texted me. It's a white male, dark blond hair, glasses. He looks clean cut, and women would find him attractive. "What's his name?"

———————————

Clarice

I LISTEN TO EVERYONE chat about how their week went, and they turn to me to ask for my story, but I play coy, acting shy, and I promise I'll tell them all about me at the next meeting, "when everyone else is back from break." Since they had already met up earlier this week, this get-together was short, nothing new to report to each other besides the fact they were bored and ready for break to be over so they could get back to work.

We all stand, exchanging pleasantries and goodbyes. I plan to walk out with a couple of the girls to try to question them, but as I go to reach out to them, Ciprian steps in front of me.

"Can I walk you out, Claire?" he asks kindly, his pretty blue eyes sparkling behind his glasses.

I glance over his shoulder, watching the others exit through the front door, and then look up at him once again. He was super nice during the meeting, encouraging each person to share their thoughts and listening intently to what they had to say. He made a great group leader, and if I actually were a foster kid who had gone off to college, I would count myself lucky to have these meetings every week. I wonder if I could get any information out of him.

"Yes, thank you, Ciprian," I reply, putting my bag over my shoulder, and he leads the way out into the parking lot.

———————

Brian

"HIS NAME IS Ciprian Mathis. He disappeared off the face of the planet for a little while after he was released, but then he started turning up in these group photos I found on both Christina and Susan's Facebook profiles. Apparently he's the head of this off-campus support group, FFKNCS—Former Foster Kids of NC State. The perfect fucking place to pick out his victims," Seth explains, and my heart sinks to my gut.

"Motherfucker!" I growl, and stomp the gas pedal to the floorboard.

"Yeah, fucked up, right?" Seth says, having no idea the reason I'm now freaked the fuck out is because I know Clarice is there, probably sitting and chatting with the fucking serial killer she's trying to gather information on.

My Clarice. I had sworn to myself never to let her get too close to my cases, to always keep her safe, and now here she is— Oh God.

His victims. Five and a half foot tall, brunette women. And knowing my girl, she probably finagled her way into the group by pretending she was also a former foster child.

"Bro, you all right?" Seth asks, hearing my tires squeal as I turn left at high speed through a red light, uncaring if police are around, as long as I get to Clarice in time.

"Seth, call the cops. I know where he is. Hartensteiner Coffee. Get them there fast!"

We disconnect, my heart pounding wildly. I've never been so fucking panicked and furious in my life. Not on deployments, with enemy fire whizzing inches from my head, not on mercenary missions, with the evilest of bastards to take out. Never. Clarice is my Achilles' heel, my kryptonite, my one and only weakness in this world, and this motherfucker is breathing the same air as her.

He might be psycho enough to believe they would let him go *again*, after already being convicted of murder before, but I know different. And even though I promised Tabitha I would take care of him myself, he deserves much worse than the swift death I'm known for doling out. The only thing I care about is getting to Clarice and making sure she's safe, and that means bringing in the closest backup I've got—the police.

Finally, I see the coffee shop at the end of the street. There's traffic at this hour, since it's around dinnertime, and I'm stuck behind several cars at a stoplight. As it turns green, my heart gives a hard thud in my chest. "Come on, come on," I rumble, feeling like I'm about to jump out of my skin with anxiety, and when I punch the gas, I breathe a sigh of relief as I make it through the light before it turns red again.

I squeal into the parking lot, looking around, and I spot her car. That's when movement catches my eye. Toward the back of the parking lot, there my girl is, being forced down into an open trunk, and my vision goes red.

If I was sure I wouldn't hurt her, I would fly across the parking lot and slam right into the motherfucker with my car, consequences be damned. But she would surely be crushed inside the trunk. That is the only reason that Ciprian Mathis will live to breathe another day.

I speed across the lot, slamming on the brakes to stop mere inches from the back of his bent body, where I see he's pulling off a piece of duct tape from a roll. He spins, his face morphing with disbelief at the car that seemed to have magically appeared behind him while he was busy *kidnapping my woman.*

My nostrils flare at the thought, and I rev the engine, staying in place with the gear in Park. His eyes widen in fear for a moment as he leans back against the open trunk. And that's when I see Clarice move. She jerks the strip of duct tape out of Ciprian's hand, squeezing it together to make it into a makeshift weapon that she immediately wraps around his throat, and I'm mesmerized watching her pull it as tight as she can. Taken by surprise, he falls backward into the trunk, and I finally snap out of it, throwing myself out of my car just as I hear sirens coming up the street.

With my six foot eight hulking frame, I easily lift Ciprian out of the trunk and off Clarice. At first, she doesn't let go of the duct tape, his head bending backward with the force of her hold as I pull him away, her face twisted and red with anger and exertion. If I weren't so fucking pissed, I would smile. Of course my girl is angry and fighting, not scared and cowering. I would expect no less from my strong-willed Clarice.

"I've got him, baby. I've got him," I soothe, catching her eyes.

With her chest heaving and her white-knuckled grip loosening, her face finally softens as she lets go just as two cop cars screech to a halt behind us.

chapter 6

Brian

I SIT ON THE EDGE OF THE BED IN OUR hotel room, my elbows on my knees as I bend forward, my head in my hands. I haven't been able to rid myself of this horrible feeling in my gut, can't erase the image of Clarice in that goddamn trunk. The vision is on repeat, alternating with flashes of Tabitha's injuries, spinning through my mind so quickly the two combine until it's Clarice's neck with the brutal-looking marks around her delicate throat. It's my girl's beautiful face marred with swollen bruises. It's her knees locked tightly together in hopes of never being separated by a man ever again.

I hear the water turn off in the bathroom as Clarice steps out of the shower. She'd asked me to join her, seeming completely unaffected by the events that happened only a few hours ago. But I couldn't. Not just yet. I needed to get myself under control, too many emotions roiling through me all at once.

Suddenly, she kneels before me, her hands coming to rest on my cheeks to lift my head from my fists. When her eyes meet mine, her face instantly morphs from jovial to shocked.

"What's wrong, big guy?" She cups my jaw, her eyes turning worried.

My brow furrows. How can she act this way? So completely unmoved by what went on in that parking lot. My voice is low when I finally speak. "Clarice." She flinches at her name coming from my lips, since I always use a pet name. "He… he almost took you," I hiss, my heart thudding in my chest.

She shrugs, shaking her head slightly, as she says, "Yeah, but you stopped him. And did you see me?" She laughs, flipping her wet hair over her shoulder. "I so could've taken him out. I would've finished him off right there if you hadn—"

"No!" I shout, cutting her off. She scoots back in her crouch, having never seen this side of me directed at her before. I soften my voice, but it's no less intense. "No, Clarice. There is no guarantee you would've been able to take him. You don't think any of his other five victims tried to escape, to fight back? He was fucking thirteen years old when he killed his foster sister. *Thirteen*. There's no telling what's been building up inside him for the last decade."

Her hand shoots to her mouth, her perfect eyebrows meeting in her horror. "So young?" she breathes.

"Yes. He had the power to kill when he was that young. Can you even imagine his ability all these years later? You saw what he did to Tabitha. You…." My words catch in my throat, and I swallow past the lump that's formed there. "You were next. You were going to be next, my love, and I would've never been able to live—"

She moves quickly, wrapping her arms around me at the sight of tears filling my eyes. "No. No, don't even think that way, Bri. You would've gotten me back some way. You would've never let anything happen to me. Even if he got me in that trunk, even if he was able to take me somewhere, I *know* you would've stopped him before he could've hurt me. I have not a single doubt about that. Not one, big guy."

My head is shaking before she finishes. "You don't know that. The only reason I was there to stop him is because of Seth. If his call hadn't come in time, you—"

"You. You would've figured it out and saved me." Her voice is so matter-of-fact that a bit of anger is able to slip in past my self-doubt and sadness. She sees my emotions change, but instead of being taken aback, this time, she looks relieved. She'd rather face my anger than see my desolation? She smiles then, her eyes smoldering as she leans forward, her breasts swelling over the top of her towel. "You solved the case, Bri. And you know what that means, don't you?" she purrs.

My nostrils flare. I want to make her understand the severity of what could've happened, but at the same time, I want to latch on to her belief in me and let her distract me from the swirl of negative feelings inside me.

"That's right." She smiles seductively. "You get your reward." She tilts her face toward me until she can whisper in my ear, her hot breath fanning over my flesh, making my cock harden instantly at her closeness. "My submission."

And as much as I want to shake her and scream in her face to make her understand what her future could've been, it dawns on me that I have a much more efficient way of getting through to her.

I stand abruptly, and she falls back on her luscious ass as I loom over her. "That's right. Get dressed. We're going to the club."

———————————

Twenty minutes later, we're inside The Stable, a BDSM club Clarice and I visited together when I was researching different clubs years ago to decide what my team and I wanted our own to be like. This was one of my favorites, and was where the idea for our different themed rooms came from.

"The cross. Naked. Now," I bark, closing the door and locking it behind me. It was one of the changes we had made at our club. Ours had curtains, ensuring no one could be locked inside with no way to escape if they needed to. But in this moment, I'm grateful no one will be able to disturb us while I dole out a punishment like I've never given before.

She briskly shoves the straps of her simple navy blue sundress off her tan shoulders, stepping out of her flip-flops as the material falls to the floor, leaving her completely naked before me. I growl, my eyes narrowing at the sight of her pantiless figure. Something else I need to reprimand her for. She smirks as she spins on her toes, her hips swaying from side to side as she makes her way over to the St. Andrew's Cross at the back of the dimly lit room, and I decide right then and there I will be turning that perfect, round ass red.

I prowl behind her, moving quietly as I veer to the right as she steps up to the cross, her head bowing like the good little submissive she is. My eyes turn to the wall of tools, and I search for the ones I'll need to make her understand what happened today is nothing to sniff at.

Unhooking them from the wall, I carry them over to her, placing them on the table so I can get her ready before we begin. I go to her right side, lifting her hand to the padded shackle at the top right of the X. Her tiny frame stretches as she goes up on her tiptoes to reach, and I take in her lightly muscled calves as I circle behind her to do the same to her left hand. When both her delicate wrists are locked in black leather, she tosses her head back, getting her hair out of her beautiful face I see before leaving her side.

Grabbing the first item from the table, I saunter up to her back, closing my eyes as she presses into my heat and savoring the feel of her softness before I lift the leather and metal over her head. I hear her swallow as I tighten the collar to an uncomfortable level, and I fasten the buckle so it'll stay that way, wound around her throat to a point she has to take slow, steady breaths in order to fill her lungs. She adjusts herself on her toes, and I go get the other two items off the table.

I move her hair out of the way, clipping the leash to the hook at the back of the collar, giving it two gentle tugs and watching her head jerk slightly with the movement. She whimpers quietly.

"You have our safeword, lover," I whisper into her ear from behind, pressing my erection into her back as my body folds around hers for a brief moment. "Do you remember what it is?" She's never used it before, so I need to know she remembers how to call everything off if this becomes too much for her. It's the only thing that will stop me from what I'm about to do to her.

She nods quickly, and then takes a slow, deep breath, trying to relax. "Afghanistan," she says quietly, the word we decided on years ago, since it was where we first met.

"Good girl." My calloused hand runs down her spine from nape to ass, and my face softens at the sight of goose bumps raising her skin. I've always loved how responsive she is to the simplest of my touches. "Now. I need you to understand. I will not be able to sleep at night until I know you grasp the danger you put yourself in, lover."

"But I do—"

I jerk on the leash, her head snapping back as she tries to gasp. "No, you don't. If you did, you wouldn't be so nonchalant about everything. You have no idea what I felt when I drove into that parking lot and saw him forcing you inside that trunk," I growl.

She nods, afraid to speak after the heat behind my words. She's never experienced a real punishment at my hands before. Only games of sexual torture. This will take our relationship—or lack thereof—to a whole new level. After the events of today, and what's about to happen, we will forever be changed. And God only knows if that will be a good or bad thing. All I know is she can't take another breath without realizing the danger she put herself in.

I loop the leash around my hand, slowly pulling her backward until she's looking up at the ceiling, her legs beginning to shake in her precarious position. And when I take my first strike against her perfect flesh, the sharp latex tails of the flogger making a loud smacking sound against the right globe of her ass, she cries out, stiffening as she lifts higher on her toes.

"As you struggle to breathe against that soft leather collar around that pretty little neck," I say menacingly, "I want you to imagine what those girls felt with that pinching, painful wire cutting into their throats." I strike her again, making her jerk forward and against the leash I hold steady. "Feel how hard it is for you to take a full breath through something cinched around your throat by someone who adores you, and then think about what it would be like having it done by someone who hates you. Someone who has only one goal. To kill you." *Smack.*

As the flogger cracks against her other cheek, she sobs, her knees trying to buckle, but the cuffs around her wrists not allowing it. I've said all I can without breaking down, imagining for myself what I instructed her to. Another word and I will lose my nerve. Instead, I take out my emotions on her beautiful ass, watching it go from smooth and tan to welted and red, listening carefully to her breathing and cries, never forgetting my responsibility as her Dom. As much as I want her to understand, I will never put her in jeopardy of truly hurting her. I have to walk the fine line of scaring her enough to learn, and scarring her psyche. And as she begins to sob steadily, and I hear her ragged breathing turn to wet sniffles, I know I've finally gotten to her.

I stop my flogging, dropping the tool to the floor as I wrap my left arm around her small body, taking her weight against my front, and I unhook the collar with my right hand. It falls to the floor as I reach up to unbuckle her hands from the cross, feeling her tremble as she continues to cry quietly.

When I've got her loose, I carry her over to the bed in one corner of the room. She curls against me, her head going limp on my shoulder. I kiss her forehead before laying her on the mattress, and when I make a move to stand, she stops me, her arms shooting around my neck to hold me close as she cries into my chest. Completely disobedient submissive behavior, but I've never seen Clarice break down like this before, so I allow it. My love for her is more important than my dominance.

"I… I'm so sorry, Bri— Knight," she corrects herself, using my Dom name, her voice portraying her sincerity. "I was j-just trying t-to be strong for y-you."

I pull back enough so I can look down into her beautiful tearstained face. "Strong for me? Why would you need to be strong for me, lover?"

"It… it wasn't your fault he was trying to take me. I thought… I thought that if I seemed like I wasn't scared of what happened, then you wouldn't feel guilty. I-I know you. You're my best friend on this earth. And I knew that if I acted anything but strong and like what went on in that parking lot didn't affect me, then you would somehow twist it into it being your fault. Whether it was because you allowed me to go talk to Tabitha, or because you missed my phone call on the way to the coffee shop, or for even just telling me about this mission at all. I *knew* it would plague you. I… I didn't want to take the chance that you wouldn't want me to meet you on your missions anymore. I didn't want to risk you saying we couldn't have our rendezvous anymore."

The last part is spoken with such panic that all ideas of punishing her evaporate. Instead, I'm filled with an overwhelming sense of love. Love I know she's still not ready to let me see. So I keep that feeling locked inside me, letting her keep her secret for a while longer. Because why else would she be so freaked out at the thought of not having our times together? Yes, we are each other's best friend, but to be willing to go to such lengths in order to keep having them? To pretend something so completely fucked up had no effect on her, just so I wouldn't try to blame myself? That's more than just the closest of friendships. That's love.

Before I even know what's happening, my hand has grown

a mind of its own, and in a blink, my jeans are unbuttoned, unzipped, and down to my knees as I bury myself deep inside her in one forceful thrust. She cries out toward the ceiling, the power of my movement sending her up the mattress. I take her arms from around my neck, capturing her wrists over her head with one of my hands, holding her down as I take her, plunging into her with animalistic fervor.

When I hear the telltale sign of her impending orgasm—her cries quieting down as she focuses her entire attention on her core, her breaths coming out in stunted pants—I pull out of her swiftly. Her whimper of disappointment fills my ears, but then quickly changes to deep, sexy moans as I move swiftly, covering her drenched pussy with my mouth. I suck at her swollen lips, relishing the musky scent and taste of her juices, and I eat her like she's my last meal.

Lapping at her clit with the full length of my tongue over and over, I feel her thighs tighten around the sides of my head as she tries to pull me even closer. I nibble the bundle of nerves with my teeth, and growl in delight at her surprised squeak before setting a pattern I know always sends her over the edge.

Her moan… deep breath… hitched pants… and then the circling of her hips as she tries to ride my face from below lets me know she's about to come. And just before she can fall over that cliff of ecstasy, I sit up on my knees, pulling my mouth away from her throbbing pussy just before I plunge deep into her once again.

Instantly, she ripples around me, her muscles clamping down on my rock-hard cock, as she screams out, "Fuck! Yes!"

My arms circle her tiny frame and scoop her up, forcing her to straddle me while I remain sitting up on my knees, impaling her as I spill inside her tight heat. My face buries in her throat and I hold her to me so tightly I'm sure she can hardly breathe, but all I can do is growl against her damp skin as jet after jet of cum fills her molten core.

We stay that way for a long moment, me gasping into her neck, savoring our closeness, and her draped around me like a living, breathing security blanket. Until finally, I stretch forward, keeping myself buried deep as I lay us down, pressing her into the mattress with most of my weight. She takes it, holding me forcefully to her, seeming unwilling to let me go.

Her voice is quiet when she breaks the silence. "Did I ruin your reward, big guy?"

I sit up enough to look into her angelic face, seeing her worried expression. "Never, lover. Every moment I get to spend in your presence is a reward. *You* are my reward," I reply sincerely, and stare mesmerized as all her concern melts from her face, leaving her relief and satisfaction on full display.

And I vow right then and there, making it my life goal to put that look on Clarice's face for the rest of our lives.

Whether she likes it or not.

The End

until we meet again

chapter 1

"**B**ro, I have a mission for you. You mind coming into my office for a minute?" Seth's voice comes over the intercom in my own office down the hall from his.

"Yeah, be there in a sec," I tell him, and hear him disconnect as I close out the paperwork I'd been finishing up from my last job.

It never gets old marking a mission Complete. Knowing another asswipe is off the streets, unable to hurt anyone else, is satisfying in a way that makes me feel like I'm actually doing some real good in this world.

For as long as I can remember, ever since the day I got out of the Army all those years ago, I've been part of a team of mercenaries. Our leader, a psychologist we all affectionately call Doc, put together our group after countless years of feeling inadequate in his job as a therapist. Yes, he was doing his part to help heal the victims of sexual assault and other horrific crimes, but after so many of his patients informed him their attackers were set free with barely a slap on the wrist, he couldn't take it anymore. Too many rapists and evil motherfuckers were getting away with shit just because their fancy lawyers spun a good enough story, some using daddy's money.

I stand and walk over to my door, and as soon as I open it, the club's thumping bass-filled music fills the hallway. I can feel the sultry beat in my chest, and it immediately makes me miss Clarice, my best friend. My secret lover. She's never been here to my club before. But maybe someday.

Besides having our mercenary team, which is hidden behind a legitimate security company, the four of us—Doc, Seth, Corbin, and I—own and run a BDSM club. It was Seth's idea in the team's beginning, worried our other business wouldn't bring in enough money for all of us, seeing how missions were few and far between. But soon, we were quite busy, word spreading of the men who acted as karma's pawns, taking out the bad guys the justice system let slip through the cracks.

I head inside Seth's office, closing the door behind me and shutting out the music, before sinking into one of his comfortable leather chairs in front of his desk. "Whatcha got for me?" I ask, ready for any excuse to get out of here.

"Job just came in from Tennessee. An old college buddy of mine I've kept in touch with, Justin, called and said they have a problem. The PI company he works for caught and put this guy away a few months ago, but—shocker—the rich bastard was able to get out," Seth says, typing away on his computer as his eyes behind his glasses move back and forth across his giant screen. It's nothing compared to his "spaceship" he's got at his place, but it still makes the computer in my office look like a Game Boy.

"Oh, thank fuck," I exhale, drawing his eyes to me.

"Not the reaction I was expecting." He lifts a brow.

"Was getting really fucking burnt out on these detective missions I've been going on lately. I'm not made to figure out *who* the bad guy is. Neck-down work is good enough for me. Point me in the direction of the motherfucker, and I'll take him out faster than you can sneeze at him. But the whole putting together clues to discover who murdered Colonel Mustard with the candlestick in the ballroom thing… to hell with that for a while," I confess, not even ashamed to admit to one of my best friends that shit is way above my pay grade. My last mission, one a couple of hours away in Raleigh, seriously did some damage to my confidence. Hopefully, getting back to what I'm really good at—murdering bad guys and making it look like an accident—will make me feel better.

He types a few more moments, and then his printer comes to life. Reaching into his desk drawer, he pulls out a manila folder and tucks the freshly printed papers inside, handing it to me with a smile. "Well, here's your silver platter, bro. This is a get-in, get-out job if I've ever seen one, and it pays damn well too. Looks like a couple of families of some of the victims pooled together to get this fuckstick a one-way ticket straight to hell," Seth tells me, and I take the folder from him before standing.

"Thanks, man."

"Careful though, Brian. Wouldn't want you to end up as a sex slave somewhere off in Eastern Europe," he warns with a chuckle.

I look back at him over my shoulder. "Sex trafficker?"

"Yup." His grin turns evil.

"Oh, this'll be fun." I match his expression before heading home to pack.

"You're actually calling me at a decent hour? What is this sorcery?" Clarice's lyrical voice fills my ear.

I'm sure she can hear the smile in my voice. "Hello, lover. I've got a job. It'll be a quick one, thank God, but I'd still love for you to meet me. Where are you right now?"

"I'm in Ashville. I just finished up a photo shoot at the Biltmore Estate for a travel magazine and was just about to go to bed before heading home in the morning. Where's your mission taking you this time, big guy?" she asks, the image of her naked form crawling beneath the hotel sheets causing me to pause and enjoy my imagination for a moment.

"Nashville. Did you drive or fly?"

"I flew. Gotta take my rental car back in the morning. I can cancel my return flight if you want to pick me up on your way through. I always get the refundable kind… since I never know when I'll be receiving these rendezvous calls." She purrs the last part, and my dick twitches at the same time my heart thumps inside my chest, knowing she keeps me in mind, anticipating the next time we'll get to see each other.

Clarice has been my best friend since we met years ago when I was deployed to Afghanistan. She's a photographer and was there documenting everything for a magazine. Our friendship blossomed to include benefits of a physical nature, and while my feelings have grown to unequivocal love—an emotion I never thought possible with my history—which I express to her in every way I can except verbally, she, on the other hand, chooses to hide her reciprocated feelings for me. Even though I can see it in her eyes every time I make love to her. Hear it in her voice every time she says my name. Feel it in my heart every time she meets me on my missions, no matter how far or inconvenient it is. The way she worries about me… it's not the worry for a friend, no matter how close the connection. It's the worry of a woman who loves a man with every fiber of her being, the way I love her.

Yet, she still isn't ready to admit it.

I glance at my watch, seeing it's only 10:00 p.m. Ashville is only four hours away. "If I leave right now, I can be to you around 2:00 a.m. I know my call came earlier than usual, but would you mind having a gentleman caller at a not so decent hour?"

She laughs, the sexy sound going straight to my cock. "Just as long as you promise *not* to be a gentleman when you get here."

Did I just come? Pretty sure my pants are wet now.

"But, beautiful Clarice. That's against our rules. I'm yours to use how you see fit until I've completed my job. And then I get to take you as my reward." As if she needs reminding. It's been this way between us for as long as I can remember. Our switch relationship—if you can call it that—is the highlight of my very being. Giving myself to the tiny, curvy, dark-haired vixen, allowing her to dominate my 6'8" hulking body any way she pleases... just knowing the pleasure I give her with my submission is enough to light up my once darkened soul. And then at the end of every job, she gifts me with her own submission. Even though I'm one of four Doms who co-own a BDSM club, she is the only woman I've been with since I met her. She's the only one I want. And until she tells me I can no longer have her, she will be the sole recipient of my domination, and she will forever be the only person on this earth to ever call me their submissive.

"True story, big guy. I'm at the Radisson, room 408. Now, I'm going to sleep until you get here. The Biltmore is freaking huge, and I'm beat. Drive safe, and I'll see you soon," she orders, just as I'm closing the door to my truck, throwing my bag in the back seat.

"Yes, ma'am," I tell her, and we end the call.

chapter 2

BY THE TIME I GET TO THE HOTEL, I'm blurry-eyed and exhausted. All I want to do is curl around Clarice's soft body and sleep until it's time to return her car. But the moment I lumber out of the elevator and to the door, her proximity hits me like a shot of adrenaline straight to my heart. I knock, and as soon as I hear her approach on the other side of the door, I'm wide awake and bracing myself for my first glimpse of her.

She opens the door, with one hand rubbing the sleep from her beautiful eyes, and when her vision is clear, her smile lights up the entire hallway as she beams up at me. "Hey, big guy," she murmurs, taking a step back to let me in.

When the door is closed, I spin us until I have her pressed against it, bending down to whisper in her ear, "Such a good girl,

Clarice. Nice to see your punishment for answering the door naked last time actually worked."

She shivers as she laughs lightly, her arms curling around my neck. "Nah, I was just freezing my tits off. I couldn't figure out how to turn the damn AC down, so I bundled up."

I growl at her sassiness, though I can't help the smile tugging at my lips. "Let me ever find out you opened a door naked without me on the other side of it, and I'll be forced to use my skills on some poor, unsuspecting delivery guy. You wouldn't want that, would you, lover?" I nibble up the column of her neck, feeling her hips jerk forward against me.

"Yeah, yeah. I know. And no more going commando under skirts. Got it. You know, you sure are bossy for not having completed your mission yet." She raises her perfect eyebrow at me, pursing her lips, which I kiss quickly before backing away.

"Pardon me." I give her a bow, placing my hand over my heart and grinning at her. When I stand to my full, towering height, I let my backpack fall off my shoulder and land at the foot of the king-size bed.

She takes a step forward, crossing her arms and sending her luscious breasts up to her collarbones. God, what I would give to press my face between them just to breathe in her scent.

"How about we play a little game?" she prompts, walking over to the bedside lamp and turning it on.

Combined with the bathroom light that was already on, I can see her perfectly clearly now, and fuck me, she's as beautiful as ever. Her long, dark hair reaches the center of her back, causing my eyes to move downward to her full, round ass that's covered in cotton pajama pants. I smile, seeing they're the ones she stole from me a few missions ago, the bottoms so long on her they pool around her feet, considering she's more than a foot shorter than me. When she turns back to face me, my gaze travels up to her hardened nipples behind her light gray tank top, just begging me to toy with them. Finally, I meet her eyes, my heart speeding when I see the mischievous look in their twinkling depths.

"What kind of game, lover? I'm surprised you aren't tying me up and forcing the details of my new job out of me." I clear my throat, trying to clear away the huskiness as I watch her approach me slowly, the sway of her hips and the bounce of her breasts like a siren's call straight to my cock.

"Who says I'm not?" She smirks, walking around me in a circle and dragging her hand around my waist as she goes. When she reaches my front once again, her fingers trail downward until she strokes my length behind my zipper, and my eyes momentarily close. "Just kidding. I won't be tying you up, but I do want those details."

When I open my eyes again, I look down into her impish face, savoring her attention. "So what kind of game?" I repeat, anxious to be inside her tight heat as she teases me.

"How about… for every detail you give me, we'll lose an item of clothing? Kinda like strip poker, but without the cards," she tells me.

"I'll see your game, and raise you. I have a folder full of not only details about the case… but photographs as well." I wiggle my eyebrows at her, watching her face light up. My crazy girl. She lives for crime shows and serial killer documentaries. Sometimes I think she keeps me around just to be close to the action.

"Deal," she chirps, and then twirls around before bouncing onto the end of the bed. She places her hands behind her and leans back on them, cocking her head to the side and giving me an expectant look.

I square myself with her as she looks up at me, and cross my arms over my chest. "The job is in Nashville. No detective work this time. Seth's old college friend, Justin, works for a private investigator slash bounty hunter, and they're paying me good money to take out someone well deserving of my skillset."

She looks me up and down, biting her full bottom lip. "Shirt," she commands with a lift of her chin.

Without hesitation, I grasp the bottom hem and lift my T-shirt over my head, watching her breasts rise and fall with a sigh at the sight of my bare chest. I love the way I affect her so easily.

"I'm glad they're paying you for this one. That last one stressed you out way too much for it to be a pro bono case. You're too giving sometimes," she scolds gently. But she has no idea what I would give to call her mine. "Continue."

"Javier Flores was kidnapping women and selling them as sex slaves in Eastern Europe. Justin and the guys were able to catch him and put him away, but he was acquitted, thanks to all the money he had hidden away and a team of the sleaziest lawyers this side of the Mississippi," I tell her.

She tilts her head to the other side. "Shoes," she instructs, and I toe off my brown leather boots, kicking them away.

This time, I don't wait for her prompt. "They've got eyes on him, watching his every move. They don't want to risk him kidnapping anyone else, so instead of waiting for him to do just that, they want me to take him out. And since a few of these women died in transit, he fits my code—life for a life."

"Jeans," she says, sitting up and tucking her legs beneath her. "How did the lawyers get him off?"

When my jeans fall to my feet, I step out of them, standing before her in only my black boxer briefs and white socks. "They were able to convince one of Flores's employees to falsely confess to the crimes, along with fake alibis for Flores himself."

She lifts her arms, pulling her hair up in a high ponytail and somehow making the movement look sensual as she uses the elastic around her wrist to keep it in place. "Hmmm. I'm going wiiith…" she draws out, before finishing, "underwear."

I shake my head and chuckle, hooking my thumbs into the top of my boxer briefs and yanking them down. When I stand back up, my erection bobs up and down, practically waving at her to draw her attention.

"Well… I guess someone else doesn't think it's chilly in this room," she breathes, eyeing my cock before lifting her gaze to mine. "Go on, big guy."

I bend over and open my backpack, pulling the manila folder out. I rifle through the contents, finding one of the photos. "Meet Javier Flores, sex trafficker who will soon be meeting his demise." I hold it out to her, and she takes it from me, giving it a close look before handing it back.

She grasps the bottom of her tank in her hands and lifts it over her head, her bare breasts swaying from side to side as she tosses her shirt down with mine. I swallow thickly before finally tearing my eyes away from her perfection to look through the folder for the next photo. "A collage of nine of the women who have been kidnapped."

Her hand traces a couple of the girls' faces, her expression turning sad for a moment before she gives the photo back to me. Suddenly, she stands, the soft flesh of her front pressing to mine as she goes up on her tiptoes and wraps her arms around my neck. "Their families will be so grateful to have you avenge their babies, Bri," she whispers, kissing the underside of my chin. "And I'm proud to call you my best friend."

I wish you would call me more than that, I think, but all daydreams are cut off as she takes a step back, hooks her fingers in the elastic of the pajama bottoms' waistband, and shoves them over her full hips, letting them fall to the floor. It leaves her completely naked before me, her hard nipples just begging to be devoured. The rest of her lightly tanned skin is covered in chill bumps, and I long to warm her with my body heat. But I have to wait for her command. If I don't, she'll make me pay for it, withholding that sweet mouth and that delicious pussy from me until she decides I've been punished enough. The vixen.

She sits on the bed and then scoots back until her legs are stretched out in front of her. I stand still, waiting for her to tell me what she wants, unknowing what's to come. Usually, she pounces like the tigress she is, taking control and riding me until she collapses. I have no idea what's going on in that pretty head of hers.

After a long moment, the tension rising between us with every breath taken, her feet slide against the comforter as she spreads her legs wide, showing me her glistening bare pussy. I weaken in the knees at the sight, but I steel my stance, giving her my submission fully by not allowing myself to give in to my feebleness. She's the only one who can do this to me. She's the only one with the power to bring this giant of a man to his very knees with merely the promise of getting to bury deep inside her.

She bites her lip when she sees my cock flex, a bead of precum at the very tip. She eyes it hungrily before meeting my eyes once again. "My, my, big guy," she purrs. "I'm famished. Why don't you come over here so we can both get something to eat?"

That's all the go-ahead I need before I shoot forward, turning around as I crawl on top of her. She takes hold of my hardness just as my knees push into the mattress above her head, and I bury my face in her drenched heat like a man starved. I groan into her depths as her lips wrap around the head of my dick, and I concentrate all my efforts on giving her pleasure with my mouth so I don't accidentally thrust down her throat. She's never topped me from the bottom before, and I'm finding it difficult not to take control in this sixty-nine position.

I suck her into my mouth, savoring the taste that is uniquely Clarice's, and feel her hands go to my ass. She digs her fingers into the muscles there, pulling me to her and then loosening her grip over and over, setting a rhythm for me to follow on my own as she moans around my shaft. My legs quiver as I try not to shove myself deep, remembering not to take my pleasure from her, but to receive what she's freely giving.

Suddenly, her knees shoot up until the tops of her thighs press into my shoulders as the practiced strokes of my tongue against her swollen clit sends her into a swift orgasm. I squeeze my eyes closed and growl against her wet flesh as she screams around my cock, forcing myself not to spill inside her mouth as she sucks ferociously. Finally, she pushes her hands against my hips and her thighs against my shoulders, signaling for me to get off her.

Within a blink of an eye, she maneuvers herself around beneath me as I hold myself up on my hands and knees. And with her breathy "Give it to me," I bury myself to the hilt inside her still throbbing pussy, relishing the vision before me as she presses her head into the bed and cries, "Brian!"

With my name on her lips and her core rippling around me, combined with how close she'd already gotten me with her devilish mouth, I thrust only once... twice... three times, before my orgasm overtakes me.

With my forehead pressed to hers as I catch my breath, I smile down at her. "That didn't take long."

She huffs out a shaky laugh. "Guess I couldn't resist you in those sexy socks."

My brow furrows, and I straighten my arms on either side of her head to turn and glance back at my still socked feet. I let out a bark of laughter, seeing the Gryffindor socks she got me for Christmas after forcing me to take some quiz online to see which Hogwarts house I would belong to.

She giggles, looking up at me with her eyes filled with adoration and satisfaction. "Now if only you wore the matching shirt I got you. I could throw it on and feel like a Hufflepuff coed who snuck into the Gryffindor hall to bang the hot Quidditch player."

With a grin, I pull out of her gently, leaning down to kiss her quickly before going to the bathroom. I bring out a washcloth dampened with warm water and clean her tenderly. Turning her around, I pull her into my body and mold myself to her back, kissing her shoulder before swiftly falling asleep.

chapter 3

We arrive in Nashville four and a half hours after dropping Clarice's rental car off at the airport. Four and a half hours of being trapped in my truck with her playing DJ and singing every single song off-key. And it was pure bliss. I would listen to that tone-deaf but sweet voice for the rest of my life. My face hurt from smiling so much—an expression I don't wear very often when she's not around.

Pausing "Hold On" by Wilson Phillips so I can hear her male British-accented Siri's navigation come over my Bluetooth, I soon pull into the small parking lot of the nondescript building that belongs to the address Seth had given me. I put the truck in Park and reach for the keys to turn it off, but pause. As much as I want her within reach at all times, I've never met these guys before. I don't want them to question my professionalism when I bring my girl— my *friend* inside with me to gather the rest of the information I need to complete my mission.

"Clar—"

"I'll wait here, Bri. No worries," she interrupts, and I love how she always seems to be able to read my mind. She looks over at me then and winks. "But you know you're gonna have to download all the new deets to me when you get back."

I undo my seat belt, lean over, and give her a peck on the lips. "Always," I reply, and then get out of the truck, leaving it running so she can listen to her music. As I walk up to the building, I hear Wilson Phillips singing their song of encouragement, with Clarice apparently yelling it at the top of her lungs, since I can hear her even with all the windows rolled up. I enter through the front door with a smirk on my face, shaking my head.

The bell above the door jingles, alerting a man of my presence, because he exits the office and greets me, "Brian?"

"That's me," I confirm.

He holds his hand out, pushing his black-rimmed glasses up his nose with the other to peer up at me. He's not short by any means, but even people who are considerably taller than average still have to look up to meet my eyes at 6'8". I reach out and shake his hand, noting the intricate tattoos covering his arms. As nerdy as his glasses are, the sleeves are badass. It's oddly like looking at Seth if he were to spend countless hours under a tattoo gun.

"Nice to meet you. I'm Justin. Seth wasn't joking when he described you as 'tall as shit,'" he tells me with a chuckle, and I follow him into his office when he turns to lead me inside. "He said he gave you all our documentation from when we were hunting Flores the first time."

"He did," I state, taking a seat in the leather chair in front of his desk as he goes to sit behind it. Before Justin can continue, we hear the bell jingle once again, and then two men enter the office, their large frames suddenly making the room feel small. I stand, assuming who these guys are, seeing how they walked in like they own the place. "Brian," I introduce myself, holding my hand out to one of them.

"Kenton," he says, giving me a solid handshake before I extend it to the other guy.

He gives it a tight squeeze in his tattoo-covered fist, rumbling, "Nico," before they both plop down on the leather couch along the wall. Years ago, before my career in the army and as a mercenary, these guys would have been intimidating as fuck. Even with all of my experience, they definitely don't seem like the type of guys one would want to fuck with. Unless one was asking for a hurting.

"All right, we're all here. Let's get this party started, shall we?" Justin speaks from behind his desk.

"Shoot," Nico orders, and Justin nods, eagerly sitting up in his chair as he turns his giant computer monitor so the entire class can see.

I shake off the déjà vu, chalking up Justin's similarities to Seth to the years they spent together in college. I vaguely remember him telling me they were roommates, but I don't recall if it was the entire time they were in school. Seth was much younger than all his classmates though—he was a child prodigy who entered MIT when he was hitting puberty—so maybe some of Justin's mannerisms rubbed off on him at such an impressionable age. Or maybe the unrestrained zeal both of them have once they put their hands to their keyboards is just a computer-nerd thing.

"Okay, so you know we put this fuckstick away a couple months ago for trafficking. He was let out two weeks ago after he was found innocent, thanks to a false confession. We've kept up with him, not taking our eyes off him since his release, since the fucker was so hard to catch the first go-round," he growls, hitting his Enter key harder than necessary. It brings up a surveillance camera feed on the monitor. "He's been keeping to a routine, not much coming or going in the last thirteen days. But he's not the kind of person to actually learn his lesson after getting caught. He's definitely the just-be-more-careful-this-time type."

We watch the fast-forwarding feed as a couple of goons come and leave Flores's ranch just outside Nashville at the same time every day. There's a grocery delivery, and one other random visit by a woman. Flores himself only makes one outing a day, to the gym fifteen minutes away from home at 11:00 a.m.

"Strange," I murmur, and Justin turns his eyes to me.

"What?"

"Well, with all that money and that big of a house, you'd think he'd have his own gym at home." I shrug.

Justin looks at Kenton and Nico. "That's true. Have you guys been monitoring his time at the gym? Is there someone he works out with every day?"

"Not that I've seen," Nico replies. "But I make sure to keep a safe distance while surveilling him, since I'm not exactly the kind of guy one forgets easily. Especially if I put you in jail." He takes off his cap and spreads his arms, showcasing all his artwork. Jesus, he must be covered neck-to-foot.

"He's never seen me before so I can get on that," Kenton inserts.

"Just give me the address of the gym and I'll handle it," I tell the room, and they all eye me. "Look, I know you've never met me before, but Justin knows Seth. And you know if Seth sent me, I'll get the job done. Been doing this shit for years, boys. Have you ever seen me on the news?" They all shake their heads. "You remember that asshole college swimmer who made national news when he raped and murdered that coed at his frat party?"

Kenton shifts on the couch. "Yeah, got off with just five minutes in the timeout chair. Had to chuckle when he turned up dead in a swimming pool. Pretty poetic."

I give him a telling look.

"That was you? Dude! I thought that was just karma coming to bite him in the ass," Justin says excitedly.

"It wasn't me, but one of my partners. I did the surveillance on that one, and he finished the job when I got called out on another mission." Ah, the one where I'd gotten to meet up with Clarice in the Florida Keys. I'd extended my stay for a couple days after I completed my job, just so I could soak up her beauty like it was the sun we laid under on the beach for hours.

Kenton and Nico turn toward each other, seeming to have a silent conversation between the two of them, until they both nod and look back to me. "I can live with that. Justin will print you out all of our new intel so you can study up and get the job done. I'm willing to hand over the case to you from here on out. It's what we're giving you this five-figure check for, I suppose," Kenton tells me, producing an envelope from his back pocket and holding it out toward me.

I put up my hand in a stopping gesture. "Hang on to that for me until the job is done."

He nods, his eyes showing a glint of respect in them. Justin speaks up, "Here you go, Brian. Everything is in here that's taken place since the last batch Seth gave you. I've already shown you everything important, his comings and goings. The rest is just the details, addresses and such." He hands me a folder, and I stand. They all get to their feet too, following me into the reception area of the office.

When I turn to tell them goodbye, Nico steps forward, looking me in the eye. I don't flinch, but a lesser man would probably cower at the serious expression on his face. "Justin told us about your code. A life for a life," he tells me, and I give him a chin lift. "This motherfucker deserves your kind of justice. Several of those girls he kidnapped died in the sea-cans he transported them in. He'd pile dozens of those poor women into a forty-foot metal shipping container, with only a few packages of bottled water and nonperishable foods, and some buckets to piss and shit in. God only knows how many died after they were sold off to the highest bidder. If anyone deserves a visit from the Grim Reaper himself, it's Flores."

With those images in my head, I give them all a curt nod. "Within twenty-four hours, he'll be taking his last breath. I won't let you guys down," I assure them.

Nico reaches out his hand to shake mine one last time. "If I didn't have my wife and kids to think about, I'd do the job myself."

I give him a small smile. "I understand," I reply, and I do. Corbin has been taking fewer and fewer missions since he remarried Vi, and because Doc and Seth are behind the scenes of our mercenary missions, they've mostly been left up to me to carry out. But the moment Clarice ever tells me she wants more than just our friendship… there'd be nothing that could take me away from her. No matter how good I am at my job, I would give it up in a heartbeat if it meant I could have her. No risk would be worth having to leave her side.

With one last grunt from Kenton, I head back out to my truck, hearing Clarice's rendition of "This is Me" from *The Greatest Showman*'s soundtrack. I had to hand it to her. If my sexy, tone-deaf girl could hit the notes, she knows the songs well enough and sang them with such enthusiasm and dramatics that she could play a part in the movie herself. She saw it six times while it was in theaters, the first time with me. And I'd held her while her eyes filled with glimmering tears that spilled down her cheeks as the bearded lady finally came out of her shell, singing and dancing her heart out. Since then, Clarice told me if she could see anyone in the world perform in person, it would be Keala Settle. I'd done research, trying to surprise her with tickets, but had come up empty on fulfilling her dream. I ended up getting her the Blu-ray as soon as it released, and she's watched it on repeat ever since.

I close the door behind me, and she turns down the music. "How'd it go?" she asks, a little out of breath from her solo car-aoke performance.

"Pretty good. I'll fill you in once we check in to our hotel," I reply, backing out of the parking space.

She claps her hand and gives me a wicked smile. "Oh, goody! Another round of Strip Clues." Her voice is both provocative and jovial.

"Damn right."

chapter 4

Less than a hundred yards from Flores's home, I'm hidden in the thick of trees that border the property as I watch the surveillance feed on my phone. Just minutes ago, a white grocery delivery van backed into his driveway, and two men in white uniforms had exited the vehicle, making their way around to the back.

They'd already made two trips back and forth, carrying brown paper grocery bags through the front door after Flores himself had answered it. After a few minutes pass, the two men exit the house and hop into their van, and the front door closes once more.

That's when something catches my eye.

Just as the van starts to make its way down the long driveway, I get a glimpse of the passenger's face. I back up the footage on my phone, zooming in. The two men who first arrived with the groceries both had facial hair—one a goatee, and the other a full beard. The man who now occupies the passenger seat, dressed in the same white uniform as the men who first showed up, is clean-shaven. And I'm sure if he took off his white ball cap, it would reveal the face of none other than Flores himself.

"Sneaky bastard knows he's being watched," I murmur, and jog to my truck parked on the side of the road on the outer edge of the trees.

Shoving the shifter into gear, I skid onto the road, knowing exactly where the van will be... and there it is. They pull out of the neighborhood, heading east. I keep a safe distance behind them, making sure not to alert them that they're being followed.

Forty-seven minutes later, I drive past the entrance of a shipping yard the van pulls into and park a distance away. Trekking back on foot, I stay in the shadows, carefully making my way around the stacked rows of forty-foot metal containers until I hear the voices of two men, one with a slight accent. But it's the words, not the voice itself, that send my hackles rising.

"Only three more? We were seven short this shipment. What the fuck are you thinking only bringing me three?" the accented voice, which I know belongs to Flores from the description in his profile, says.

"Sorry, boss, but with the curfew still in place, the... product has been harder to acquire," the other man explains, fear lining his tone.

"Well then, you're going to have to be more creative. There

are many ways to acquire what we need during the day. You'll just have to be more careful about it," Flores growls, and I realize I'll have not one, but two murdering assholes to take care of tonight. If this other man is the one kidnapping the girls who end up dying during transport and after, then he's just as responsible for their deaths as his employer.

As their back and forth continues, I creep closer, now hearing muffled whimpers coming from the vehicle, and my stomach goes tight. There are girls in the back of the goddamn van! And suddenly, this has turned into a rescue mission.

"Show me the others. We ship tonight. Saxton will be here in an hour. Same as always, he'll load the sealed and marked container onto his eighteen-wheeler, and it'll be loaded onto the ship by morning once he reaches the coast. I will dock your pay for the missing four. But next time? There will be no next time," Flores warns, and as I make my way to the end of one of the stacks, I peek around to see their retreating backs as they disappear behind another.

I sprint on silent feet to the back of the van, hoping like hell it's unlocked, but of course it's not. Glancing around the side of it, I see the driver side door is open. *Bingo!* I yank the keys out of the ignition and hurry to unlock the handle before twisting it and pulling the door open.

My heart seizes at the sight before me.

Three terrified faces of young women stare back at me. Their hands are duct-taped behind them, and their mouths are taped shut. Tear-streaked dirt covers their cheeks, but for the most part, they look externally unscathed.

I lift myself into the back of the van and pull my knife out of my pocket, trying to ignore the panicked intakes of breath from the petrified girls. I need to focus on getting them free and listening out for Flores and his goon, but know I should reassure them.

"It's okay. I'm not going to hurt you," I whisper, cutting the duct tape from around one of the women's wrists. I don't waste time with the piece across her face; she can do that herself while I work on getting the others loose. When I'm finished, I tell them, "You're free to run, but we're miles from anything. I'll get you to safety, but I have to do something about the men who took you first. Either way, you never saw me. Understand?" I meet each of the girls' eyes, trying to convey with a look the importance that they never mention me.

The brunette on my left speaks up quietly. "That's the guy from the news, the one who's been running the sex trafficking ring. They let him go a couple weeks ago."

"I kno—"

"I heard them say there are more women here somewhere. We've gotta save them," the blonde to my right says.

"That's what I'm here to do," I assure her, even though that's not quite the whole truth. "Here are the keys to the van. I'll take care of everything. When I get the others free, get everyone to safety. Go straight to the hospital. I just need your promise that you never saw me. One of you were able to get the tape off and helped the others get free. You don't know what happened to the guys who took you. Got it?"

"Yes, sir," the third girl says, and the others nod their agreement. "We know what happened to the women he took before. We owe you our lives. We won't say a word."

"All right. No matter what you hear, do not come looking," I order, and with one last nod from the girls, I turn and hop out of the van, closing the doors behind me quietly but leaving a crack so they know they're not trapped.

I run up to the nearest stack of shipping containers, turning to press my back against the cool metal as I glance around the end. At the far end of the yard, I see the two men dressed in white. The goon is holding a gun aimed inside the open door of a rusted dark-red container, while Flores checks something off on a clipboard, glancing up every few seconds to look inside.

Hurrying to the opposite end of the one I'm hiding behind, I swiftly make my way up the column of containers until I'm on the same row as Flores. With so many witnesses, I have to be fast and think about how to do this without any of the girls inside the container seeing me. Three, I can trust not to say anything about me. But who knows how many are in there, and for how long? Many could be on the verge of a psychological break. I can't risk anyone giving my description to the police.

"Here goes nothing," I murmur to myself, and I rear back and kick the metal container I'm hiding behind with my steel-toed boot. In the quiet of the night, it makes a light gonging noise. It's not very loud, since the metal is thick, but it's just enough to have Flores spinning around to look in my direction. From his position though, he would be looking into pitch darkness, since there isn't one of the huge lights on this column. It's on his.

"Did you hear that?" he asks his man. And just as I was hoping, he orders, "Go check it out." The other guy turns toward me, pulling his aim away from the women inside the container.

I watch as Flores closes the metal door and locks it, so I'm safe from being seen by so many eyes. He slips the clipboard into a pouch attached to the lock, which I assume is the marking he mentioned before. Even though I'd love nothing more than to take care of the Saxton person who carries out the shipping aspect in Flores's trafficking ring, I need him to do his job one last time.

As the goon approaches cautiously, his weapon leading the way, I get into position, ready to take him out first. Just as the black revolver appears from around the corner, my hands shoot out, pulling the fucker out of the row and slamming him up against the back of the shipping container so swiftly that he drops the gun. My grip wraps around his throat, shutting off his ability to scream… and breathe. My hand, nearly the size of a dinner plate, feels like it could snap the man's neck like a twig, and within a minute, he no longer has a pulse. I drop him to the ground, kicking his gun behind him as I hear Flores approaching.

"Jefferson?" he calls out. "Did one of them get free?"

Of course that's what he thinks. He believes he's been entirely too sly with the whole deliveryman switch to worry about anyone else being here besides the women they kidnapped. Well, he's in for a rude awakening.

Just as he rounds the corner, I allow him just enough time to see his man on the ground, crumpled at his feet, and I take pleasure in the shocked expression that takes over his face as his eyes lift, lift, and lift some more, until he meets mine. He pales in the dim light, and a smirk lifts one corner of my lips as I jerk him forward, spinning him just before wrapping my arm around his neck.

It almost seems unfair, the difference in our sizes. It's like holding an adolescent he's so much smaller than me, but then I remember what he's spent the last several years doing, kidnapping women and selling them overseas to the highest bidder, causing the deaths of countless innocent victims, and I no longer feel the twinge of guilt. With little effort, I feel the fight and then the life leave Flores's body, and I allow him to fall to the ground. Bending down, I pull the keys from his pocket.

Leaving the two men there, I hurry back to the van, opening one of the doors. The girls' faces fill with relief when they see it's me. "I need one of you to take these keys and go free the other women. I can't allow them to see me. Too many witnesses who could release a description of me."

"Are the men…?" the brunette asks shakily, and I nod. "I'll do it." Her voice steadies, and she reaches her hand out.

When I place the keys in her palm, I help her from the back of the van. "Leave them in the lock once the women are out. It'll be a tight squeeze, but everyone should be able to fit in the van. Go straight to the hospital," I instruct. "It's the last container on the left. A rusty red color. Leave the clipboard."

"Got it," she says, and she turns but pauses. Spinning back around, her arms wrap around my waist tightly for a brief hug. "Thank you, whoever you are."

I can't help my smile as a feeling of accomplishment fills me. Mine is normally a thankless job, one of avenging those who are already gone from this earth. It's with great pride I murmur, "You're welcome," before I send her on her way with a light pat on her back.

I give the other two girls inside the van a salute before I disappear into the shadows. I watch with satisfaction as nearly all of the women inside the container burst into tears of relief as they see it's the brunette struggling to open the heavy metal door and not the men who took them. "We're free!" she tells them. "Go to the van! Hurry!" And my heart thuds in my chest as all of them empty out of their cage, some holding hands for support, while others haul ass towards safety.

When I hear the doors of the van slam shut and the ignition start, I wait just a few moments to make sure they're gone before I get to work. Bending down, I feel for a pulse on each of the men, not taking any chances. But I have nothing to worry about, because they're already going cold.

I haul their bodies into the shipping container that once held the women they planned to sell as slaves, closing the door and locking it with the keys the brunette left just like I asked. And several minutes later, just like Flores said, I watch as the container is loaded onto an eighteen-wheeler and disappears into the night, hopefully never to be opened again until it arrives at its overseas destination.

chapter 5

"ACCORDING TO OUR GUY, THE CONTAINER wasn't opened before the ship departed. We'll continue to follow up and hope it fizzles out without their boss, but knowing the money that's in sex trafficking now, more than likely, one of the lower guys in Flores's ring will take over. All we can do is be vigilant about keeping up with them, cutting them off at the quick before they can make a shipment," Justin tells me, and I run my hand through my hair.

"Job well done, Brian. Here's that check you told me to hang on to for you," Kenton says, and I take the payment from his outstretched hand, fold it up, and stick it into my back pocket.

"I gotta say though, bro. You didn't make it look like an accident," Justin points out.

"I figured the people opening the container expecting to find a bunch of young women to sell as sex slaves wouldn't exactly be the types to go running to the police to tell them they found two dead bodies instead." I shrug.

He chuckles and leans back in his chair. "Fair enough."

"Got a question for you guys. Might sound a little strange," I warn.

"Shoot," Nico prompts, putting his elbows to his knees as he sits forward and links his tattooed fingers together.

"Never been to Nashville before. Do you know of any reputable establishments around here like mine?" I ask, and they all grin.

"A club of the kinky persuasion?" Justin clarifies.

"Yep."

"Makes sense. Nothing like offing scumbags to get the mortality juices flowing, am I right?"

"Something like that," I reply.

"I know just the man to call," Kenton says, and pulls out his cell. He hits a button before setting it on Justin's desk, and the ringing sound comes through the speakerphone.

"What's up?" a deep voice answers.

"Kai, you know any good BDSM clubs in Nashville?" Kenton asks, and the man on the other end of the call chuckles.

"Does Autumn know about this?" he responds.

"Not for me, motherfucker. Friend of mine is visiting from North Carolina. He owns one there and... needs his fix," Kenton explains, his eyes shifting to me.

"I've got a buddy who runs one there. If his nightclub in Vegas is anything to go on, then it'll be nice as fuck. I mean, not as nice as mine, but ya know. Only thing is, I don't think they let single men in. Only single women and couples," Kenton says, his voice sounding regretful.

"I won't be alone," I speak up, and Justin holds out his fist toward me.

"Daps, my man," he tells me, but then his face screws up. "Wait… it's not one of the chicks you rescued, is it? That would seem… wrong. Like taking advantage—"

"Fuck off. Of course not. My girl is back at the hotel." I shake my head, then turn to Kenton. "I'd appreciate that information."

"Club Sybian is the name. You'll see why when you get there." We exchange goodbyes, and the call disconnects.

Kenton holds out his hand to me. "It was cool meeting you. If we ever need your skillset again, we won't hesitate to call. Thank you for taking care of the problem so quickly."

"No worries. You've got our number," I say, shaking his hand and making my way to the door as I give Justin and Nico a chin lift.

Now, I've got a much more pleasurable reward to collect.

chapter 6

"Oh, fuck," Clarice murmurs, as we pull into the parking lot of the BDSM club. On the way back to the hotel to pick her up, I called Seth, and he did some swift research for me to make sure this place was up to par. A dirty little hole in the wall would never do for my girl, and seeing that the club I owned is ranked one of the top three in the country by the BDSM community, I'm a bit of a club snob myself, spoiled by our rules and standards. Thankfully, Kai hadn't steered us wrong.

I chuckle at her reaction when she sees the name of the club. "Just wait," I tell her mischievously, my eyes twinkling when she meets them with her half-excited, half-nervous ones.

"Goddamn it, Bri. Don't you remember what happened the first time you put me on one of those things? I couldn't even fucking walk afterward. You had to carry me for the rest of the night!" she complains.

I smirk. "Oh, I remember. It was fucking awesome." I laugh as she swats my chest with the back of her hand.

"Awesome, my ass," she grumbles.

"That was years ago. Maybe your tolerance is higher now."

"Maybe your tolerance is higher now," she mocks in a sneering voice, unbuckling her seat belt.

Quick as a cobra strike, I hook the back of her head in my palm and pull her toward me, my voice dropping low as my fingers sink into her scalp. "Keep it up, lover. I'd love nothing more than to punish you like last time. I had a lot of fun turning your ass red in Raleigh."

She swallows thickly, her eyes turning dark and lustful. "Sorry, Knight." She whispers my Dom name, remembering it's my turn to dominate since I completed my mission.

"Good girl. Now let's go." I give her a quick kiss on the lips before letting her loose.

She's my perfect submissive after that, staying slightly behind my towering frame as we register. My business's reputation precedes me, allowing us free access to a private room once the woman at the door sees I wrote Owner next to my club's name under Membership. This happens pretty often. Other clubs hope I will recommend their establishment to anyone who asks, since mine is so highly acclaimed. Word of mouth is our community's most important form of advertising.

I take Clarice's hand, and she looks up at me, surprised. A lot of Doms don't hold hands with their submissive, because it's a show of equality between them and their partner. I usually don't do it, just because Clarice is funny about PDA, especially since we aren't officially in a relationship. Even when it's my turn to be the dominant, I don't force the show of affection, knowing it makes her uncomfortable. But as we entered the main part of the club, it was my instinctive reaction to take hold of the woman I know in my heart is mine.

The space is crowded, three times as busy as my club on any given night, which is saying a lot. But we're also in a much bigger city than the small military town in which I live. Seeing the room we're assigned on the back wall, I head that way, keeping a tight grip on her tiny hand as we weave through the masses. The bass of the music thumping in my chest, and the swirling lights, strobes, and lasers, irritate my senses, making it hard to breathe. My blood pressure rises as the bodies brush against me, and knowing they're touching my Clarice, as I pull her through the crowd, makes my pulse quicken until every muscle in my body is tense and ready to strike out.

Finally, I breathe a sigh of relief once we're closed inside our private room.

I feel Clarice's soft palm on my stubbled cheek and realize I closed my eyes once I'd shut us in. When I meet her worried gaze, the anxiety caused by the ruckus out there leaves me. "You okay, big guy?" she whispers, my sweet girl coming out of her submission as she presses her front to mine, knowing her closeness always calms me.

I allow myself to soak in her warmth, feeling the tension leave my body. After a few minutes, I stand up straighter and nod, giving her a reassuring smile. "All good, lover. Let's begin," I say quietly, and she steps back once more after giving me a quick sultry grin, returning to her submission like she'd never come out of it. After giving her the command, we both undress quickly, lust crackling the air between us. Wanting to touch her, I reach out and take her hand, leading her over to the device the club was named after.

"During my research of this place, I discovered a lot of the equipment here is handmade by some of the talented members. Each private room contains a Sybian, but the attachments and other devices in the rooms vary. I chose this one, because of this particular setup," I tell her, stroking the cold metal of the frame standing over the saddle-shaped vibrating machine.

I watch as her eyes take in the modern-day stocks the club owner himself welded, her gaze filling with heat. Once a submissive is placed within its grasp, they won't be able to move their upper body whatsoever. But there's a surprise in store I'm not willing to share quite yet.

Taking hold of one side of the metal arm, I open the stocks, the metal hinge not making a sound as it swings open. "Kneel over the Sybian, facing me," I order, and my cock flexes as I see her position her perfect, bare pussy on the ribbed rectangle along the top of the saddle. "Arm's up."

She lifts her arms, and I place my hand at her throat, gently pressing her backward until her neck fits into the crevice of the stocks, before positioning her wrists in their spaces. Slowly, I close the metal arm, which is a mirror image of the back one she's pressed against, and the stocks lock together, holding her in place. Although the stocks had been invented centuries ago, never has there been a more beautiful prisoner as I have before me now.

I stroll behind her, watching her take steadying breaths to calm her nerves, since she can't turn to see what I'm doing. Yet she knows very well what comes next. Taking hold of the remote attached to the Sybian she's mounted, I take pity on her and turn the vibrations on using the lowest setting. Still, she gasps and her hips jut forward, her hands balling into fists where they are trapped.

"That's right, lover." I get to my knees behind her, leaning down to whisper in her ear. "Ride it. Grind those sexy hips and fuck it until you come."

I turn the speed up and fight back a groan as I watch her ass flex and relax before she starts to give in to the inevitable. Even though I've seen her in reverse cowgirl position countless times, it never gets old watching her full hips and round ass move in their hypnotic way. Shakira has nothing on my Clarice.

Clicking the vibrations up once more, she cries out, her body shuddering as the machine suddenly forces her into a quick orgasm she can't hold back. "That's it," I breathe into her hair, reaching around her body to trail my fingers up her soft stomach to cup her full breast in my palm. She whimpers as the Sybian continues to vibrate from below, and I glance down to see her thighs quivering around the saddle. That's when I decide it's time to show her just what else the metal she's trapped within can do.

Taking hold of the metal legs on either side of us, I use my thumbs to depress the two buttons at the same time, and Clarice moans as her upper body is suddenly bent forward. Her clit now presses into the Sybian at a new angle as the legs lock in a ninety-degree angle. I can only image what she feels right now, almost as if she's floating face-down over the floor, as the machine pulls wave after wave of torturous pleasure from her body.

Moving forward on my knees, I line up with her glistening slit, and slowly, I sink into her, feeling her ripple along my length as she continues to come. She sobs, "Yes!" and I grip her hips, my fingers digging into the succulent flesh. My eyes roll back as my balls slide along the vibrations of the saddle beneath us, soaked with her juices, while I thrust into her over and over again.

Knowing she can't take much more, her pleasured cries of passion now punctuated by panicked squeals, my brow furrows in concentration as I bury myself to the hilt, allowing her soaked pussy to milk the orgasm from my throbbing cock. My big body folds over her tiny frame, engulfing her as I bury my face between her shoulder blades and growl. I come long and hard as her lower half grinds back against me, until finally, I can't take anymore. I use the remote to turn off the machine, and her body melts beneath me, yet still unable to move thanks to the stocks.

I take a deep breath of her, savoring her unique scent that never fails to soothe my soul. And when I can finally force myself, I slip from her depths. Taking hold of the metal legs, I sit her back up, the stocks locking back into their upright position. She's still panting as I stand, wobbling slightly on my feet for a moment as the room spins. "Fuck, lover. I think I might need to invest in this setup," I tell her, unlocking the arm and allowing it to swing open and free her from her confines.

She doesn't seem to be able to move, just like the first time we played with a Sybian years ago, so I bend down and pick her up, lifting her into my arms as her curvy body molds to my front. I walk over to the leather couch against the wall, sitting down with her in my lap, and relish the closeness.

What I would give to be able to hold her like this every night. To feel every day this soul-deep connection that's so blatantly obvious between us during aftercare.

Knowing her walls will soon be erected once again, I use the few moments we have left of this feeling to kiss her gently. Each of her closed eyelids gets a soft peck, causing a small smile to appear on her lips, so they get the next press of my mouth. When I feel her fingertips along my bearded jaw, my eyes meet hers, and for a split second, I see the love I feel for her reflected in their depths.

I hold my breath, my heart thudding in my chest.

Will she finally say it? Will she finally admit to feeling more, so much more than friendship between us? I know it's there. I see it dancing in her pupils like a clumsy little girl spinning in a bed of wildflowers, her footing unsure but uncaring as she gets dizzier the more she turns. The feeling is uncomfortable and exhilarating at the same time.

But she must see I'm catching on to her feelings, because suddenly, she blinks, and a sultry grin spreads across her perfect face as my heart sinks a little knowing her protective walls are back in place.

"I have to admit, if you invest in that setup, I might just have to come visit your club," she purrs, and my heart peeks out from where it had fallen.

"You say the word, lover, and my place is yours."

The End

club sorcery

Clarice

BRIAN SMIRKS AT ME, that same delicious look he gives me every time he has something wicked planned. I tilt my head back to look up at the shackles he placed around my wrists only moments ago. Instead of raising the chains to pull me up on my tiptoes like he's done many times before, he left me flat-footed, and it makes me nervous. What's in store for me that he wants me to be in full control of my balance?

My face lowers, and I gasp as I take in his broad, muscular chest so close to me. I hadn't heard him move. My eyes lift to meet his as he towers over me, making me feel tiny, which I am, compared to him. He could break me so easily, yet all he ever does is build me up, making me feel like his own personal queen.

His laughing eyes take in my surprise at his closeness, and his smirk widens into a grin as I watch in shock as he floats backward, his feet unmoving.

"Wha—" I breathe, my gaze flitting from his black boots to above his head, looking for either a conveyor belt or ropes, anything that could possibly explain how he moved away from me without taking so much as a step in that direction.

"Club Sorcery, lover. One can do all sorts of things here that they can't outside these walls." His deep voice slides over me like satin, making my exposed nipples pebble at the suggestion I hear in its depths. He punctuates his words by holding his hand out in front of him, waving it slowly in an S, and even from feet away, I feel his touch as it caresses down my torso.

He smiles and adds his other hand, spreading his fingers as his lips start to move silently. I jump in my restraints, moaning out in surprise as it feels as if four… five… even six hands move across my skin. I look down to make sure no one has slipped into our private room at the BDSM club Brian brought me to after the mission he just completed. No one is there. I expect to see my breasts being pushed up and squeezed, the way it feels as I take in the sensations, but they're not. From Brian's perspective, I would just look like a good little submissive, hanging here waiting for him to do with me as he pleases. But I swear I feel his two palms circling my nipples. I feel two more sliding around my hips to grip and squeeze my ass. There's another slipping down my stomach, over my mound. And yes, there's his long, thick finger teasing between my folds.

My gaze meets his once more, and my knees buckle at his hungry expression just as I feel something enter me. I focus on his hand gestures, letting his light murmurs of a language I don't understand wash over me. I watch as he says something over his left shoulder, and I squeak as the chair that was up against the back wall moves by itself, appearing behind Brian just as he sits down.

I have no time to question it before I'm quickly overcome with sensations between my spread legs. And I know now why he left me flat-footed.

"We use Hitachi Magic Wands all the time. But you've never felt anything until you've experienced a *real* magic wand," he says as a slender object I can't make out very well in the dim lighting appears in his hand. I cry out as vibrations overwhelm my core. I feel it deep inside me at the same time it envelops my clit. It's as if my entire pussy is the focus of his magical ministrations, not just a specific part, and the back of my neck begins to sweat.

"I can't—" I try to warn him I won't be able to stop the orgasm rushing up to greet me, when suddenly everything stops. Not even a lingering mystical hand on my breast. "That was…" I pant, looking to where he still sits in the chair far in front of me.

"Yes, lover?" he prompts.

"…fucking *mean*!" I finish, glaring at him.

He chuckles then snaps his fingers, and I gasp once more as he disappears. It's only a moment later when I scream bloody murder as I feel his lips against my backside. I twist as much as I can without hurting my wrists to see he's now sitting behind me, looking up at me with that playful look I love so much.

He stands, and I shiver as he presses his hulking frame against me. The invisible hands from before felt wonderful, but nothing could compare to Brian's body covering me from head to toe, engulfing me with his controlled strength.

"Mean?" he breathes into my ear, making me shiver. "You'd rather come with me all the way across the room? Or do you want more?"

I press back into him, rising to my tiptoes so my ass fits against his massive erection. "Always more," I murmur, my head tilting back to rest on his chest, wanting to be ever closer.

"That's what I thought."

Before I realize what's happening, my hands are free from their shackles, and I'm floating. I try to struggle in my panic as my legs rise and my body falls backward, but I can't move anything but my head. My eyes lock with Brian's as I discover his lips moving the way they were before, and I relax, understanding it's him putting me into whatever position he wants me in.

I'm laid out flat when I come to a stop, as if I'm lying on a bed, my hands resting above my head, my body stretched out, breasts lifted to the ceiling as Brian comes to stand next to me.

"So many possibilities. What shall I do with you, my little witch?" he taunts.

My eyebrow quirks. "Witch? Is that what this place makes you?"

He furrows his brow. "Fuck if I'd let anyone call me a witch, accurate or otherwise."

I smile up at him. "Warlock then? Or how about a wizard? Should I start calling you Harry instead of Knight for your new Dom name?" I cry out as I feel a sharp smack against my ass, and I squint haughtily at his unmoving form before remembering my place as his submissive.

He tilts his head to the side and gives me a sexy grin. "I think we'd both agree I'm more… a superhero."

I nod as much as he allows. "Definitely. You'd fit in more with the Avengers than at Hogwarts. Superhero it is then."

My legs part and bend at the knees as Brian moves between my floating feet. As he starts to chant in that unknown language, the wet lapping of a tongue against my center makes my breath whoosh out of me as all thoughts of Marvel characters leave my brain. My eyes close as the nimble, invisible tongue sets a rhythm against my clit, only to open in surprise as I'm filled to the brim by a cock that feels as if it were made for me. But this is no magical manifestation. That perfect, breathtaking rod is attached to the beautiful man pumping in and out of me, his lips never stopping their lyrical mantra as he thrusts.

I don't even know what to call the sounds coming out of me as the licking at my clit increases in speed and Brian pounds even deeper. I'm vaguely aware my throat is beginning to feel raw from my screams mixed with moans and gasps. And when I think the sensations wracking my body can't become anymore overwhelming, Brian bends forward, taking one nipple into his mouth as he continues to speak his magical spell around it. I cry out as a second mouth emulates what his is doing to my other nipple, driving me quickly to the point of insanity, not knowing what to focus on. Brian's cock driving into me at a punishing rate and depth. The mind-numbing suction of the mouth on my clit. Or the teeth, lips, and tongues doing sinful things to both of my breasts. So instead, I give in to it all, letting it all overtake me, and with one final thrust…

I shoot up in bed, my breath coming out of me in sharp pants. I take in my surroundings the best I can in the dim lighting, but see I'm in a hotel room. Someone beside me rolls over to look at me, and it takes me a second to realize it's Brian.

"You okay?" he asks sleepily.

I push my long hair out of my face, feeling the sweat at my temples at the same time I become achingly aware of the throbbing between my legs. I let out a soft chuckle, kicking the sheet off of me before pushing him onto his back and straddling his already hardening cock.

"Better than okay. I just had the strangest dream," I confess.

"Oh yeah?" He smiles lazily. "What about?"

"Well, I'd just show you what happened, but it would require you and about three or four other people—"

He growls, and I love the look of possessiveness on his face as he becomes fully awake.

"No worries, big guy. Unless you've got a magic wand that can conjure a bunch of disembodied mouths and hands, the best part of my dream was when you took your big cock—" I grab hold of his erection and guide him to my center. "—and fucked me until I couldn't breathe."

I squeal as he rolls us over faster than I can blink. "Lover, I don't need a magic wand to do that."

And he spends the next hour taking my breath away.

Acknowledgements

This bonus scene was supposed to be part of a story I was writing for Robyn Peterman's Magic and Mayhem World. It was because of her panel and her hilarious stories that the idea to take Brian and Clarice on an adventure to a paranormal BDSM club popped into my head. Unfortunately, KW closed before it could be released, but I'm so happy I got to meet and now support one very talented PNR romance author! Thank you, Robyn, for everything.

Also, thank you, Michele Bardsley for letting me follow you around like a smitten kitten, which led me into that panel. I still get teary-eyed when I watch the video of getting to hug you for the first time! Love you, lady!

About the Author

KD Robichaux wanted to be a romance author since the first time she picked up her mom's Sandra Brown books at the ripe old age of twelve. She went to college to become a writer, but then married and had babies. Putting her dream job on hold to raise her family as a stay at home mom, who read entirely too much, she created a blog where she could keep her family and friends up-to-date on all the hottest reads. From there, by word of mouth, her blog took off and she began using her hard-earned degree as a Senior Editor for Hot Tree Editing. When her kids started school, and with the encouragement from her many author friends, she finally sat down and started working on her first series, The Blogger Diaries, her very own real life romance.

Join her reader group on FB:
KD-Rob's Mob

Made in the USA
Coppell, TX
04 June 2022

78477191R00098